"I heard a suspicious click right before the explosion. Someone wants you dead—with no evidence left behind."

"If you hadn't been here—"

She gripped his shirt and buried her head against him. He'd seen the reaction before. He held her tight.

"We'll find out who's doing this. I promise."

She wrapped her arms around his neck and hugged him tightly. He couldn't say no to her trembling frame. Each shudder evoked every protective instinct throbbing in his veins. He cradled her against him and stroked her hair softly, brushing a few stray snowflakes out of her hair. "You're okay. It'll be okay."

He was lying. Again. This assassin wanted a kill. Mitch could stop him only so long—unless he discovered who was behind the attempts on her life.

ROBIN PERINI

FINDING HER SON

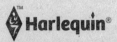

TORONTO NEW YORK LONDON
AMSTERDAM PARIS SYDNEY HAMBURG
STOCKHOLM ATHENS TOKYO MILAN MADRID
PRAGUE WARSAW BUDAPEST AUCKLAND

For my mom—the most ferocious mama bear I know. Your love and unbending faith in me have given me the strength to persevere. I am truly blessed. I love you, Mom. Always.

Acknowledgments

I'm living my dream. But no one gets to this wonderful place alone.

To my amazing editor, Allison Lyons, who saw something in my writing and took a chance. You made my dreams come true.

To the most vicious critique group ever—Tammy Baumann, Louise Bergin and Sherri Buerkle. I love you all. You, my dear friends, sacrificed for this one more than anyone will know. I am humbled and grateful. Let's not do it again!

To Angi Platt and Jenn Stark for their keen insight and willingness to help. Thanks are not enough, and I expect payback.

To my best friend and the sister of my heart, Claire Cavanaugh, the wind beneath my wings. This book wouldn't be here without you. You know why.

PLEASE RECYCLE

THIS PRODUCT IS RECYCLABLE

Recycling programs for this product may not exist in your area.

ISBN-13: 978-0-373-69607-9

FINDING HER SON

Copyright © 2012 by Robin L. Perini

www.Harlequin.com

Printed in U.S.A.

ABOUT THE AUTHOR

Award-winning author Robin Perini's love of heart-stopping suspense and poignant romance, coupled with her adoration of high-tech weaponry and covert ops, encouraged her secret inner commando to take on the challenge of writing romantic suspense novels. Her mission's motto: "When danger and romance collide, no heart is safe."

Devoted to giving her readers fast-paced, high-stakes adventures with a love story sure to melt their hearts, Robin won the prestigious Romance Writers of America® Golden Heart® Award in 2011. By day, she works for an advanced technology corporation, and in her spare time, you might find her giving one of her many nationally acclaimed writing workshops or training in competitive small-bore rifle silhouette shooting. Robin loves to interact with readers. You can catch her on her website, www.robinperini.com, several major social-networking sites or write to her at P.O. Box 50472, Albuquerque, NM 87181-0472.

Books by Robin Perini

HARLEQUIN INTRIGUE

All backlist available in ebook. Don't miss any of our special offers. Write to us at the following address for information on our newest releases.

Harlequin Reader Service
U.S.: 3010 Walden Ave., P.O. Box 1325, Buffalo, NY 14269
Canadian: P.O. Box 609, Fort Erie, Ont. L2A 5X3

CAST OF CHARACTERS

Emily Wentworth—Desperate to find her son, she can't trust the Denver police. But can she trust the cop who saved her life?

Mitch Bradford—The injured SWAT cop has been reassigned to prove Emily's guilt in her husband's death. Will he sacrifice everything to protect a murder suspect and help her find her son?

Eric Wentworth—He had secrets worth killing him for, but he hadn't meant to sacrifice his wife and son.

Joshua Wentworth—Why was he stolen from his mother at just one month old?

Kayla Foster—Can Emily find this missing, pregnant teen before it's too late?

Perry Young—Is Emily's alcoholic investigator making mistakes, or is he involved?

Victoria Wentworth—Eric's mother never accepted Emily and believes her daughter-in-law is responsible for his death. Does she want revenge?

Dane Tanner—Why is this Denver police detective so determined to prove Emily's guilt?

William Wentworth—Emily's brother-in-law bankrolls her investigation to find her son. Will his parents force him to abandon her?

Ghost—This mysterious criminal has an interest in desperate pregnant women. Did he take Emily's son, as well?

Thomas Wentworth—How far did Eric's father go to get his son back into the family business?

Noah Bradford—Mitch's brother mysteriously shows up with secrets of his own.

Prologue

Icy wind howled through the SUV's shattered windshield, spraying glass and freezing sleet across Eric Wentworth's face. He struggled in and out of consciousness. Flashes of memory struck. Oncoming headlights on the wrong side of the road. Skidding tires on black ice. The baby's cries. Emily's screams.

Oh, God.

Why couldn't he focus? Above the wind, he heard only silence, then an ominous gurgling sound from his lungs. He shifted his head slightly to check on his wife, and a knife-like pain seared his neck. He stopped, staring in horror at the shaft of metal guardrail penetrating his chest. Blood pulsed from the wound, but he couldn't feel it. He couldn't feel anything.

Eric was dying. And it was no accident. He hadn't taken the threats seriously, hadn't told Emily what he'd done. Why they were all in danger.

"E-Eric?" Her voice was weak, barely audible over the storm gusts.

Thank the Lord she was still alive. In the darkness, he could just make out her small frame pinned by the dashboard. He had to warn her.

Emily. Escape. Before he comes back.

No sound came from his lips, and at the effort, his vision blurred.

"Eric, are you all right?"

Fear tinged her voice, but he could do nothing to comfort or reassure her.

A soft cry came from the backseat. The baby. Only a month old.

"Mommy's here." Emily pushed at the dash. "Eric, I'm stuck. I can't get to Joshua."

Headlights swept across the crumpled interior. A vehicle pulled up behind them.

"A car! Help!" Emily called out. "We're trapped! There's a baby in here!"

No! Emily. Get out. Now. Please. Take Joshua. Run.

A door slammed, but from the stealth of the approaching footsteps, Eric knew this was no rescue. Tears of impotent rage scalded his cheeks. *They're innocent. Don't kill them. They've done nothing.*

The back door ripped open, revealing a dark, hooded figure. The baby whimpered. After a moment's hesitation, the person unclicked the car seat and yanked it free.

The baby's cries filled the air.

A sob escaped Emily's throat. "Joshua? Is he all right?"

Without responding, the man shined the flashlight through the broken passenger window, scanned Emily, then focused the blinding light directly in Eric's face, illuminating his fatal wounds.

Emily gasped. "Eric! No! Please. Please, help my husband."

Struggling to remain conscious, Eric stared toward the beam of light, willing the man not to carry out the contract, silently begging for mercy for his family.

As if in answer, the man reached into the car, grabbed Emily and slammed her head on the door frame. With quick movements, he wrapped her hand around a jagged piece of windshield and forced it to slash across her neck.

No. Not Emily! Eric's silent scream echoed her agonized one. The man slammed her head again. She fell silent. Blood trickled down her throat.

With one last mocking salute, the bastard lifted the baby's car seat and turned away, smearing blood across the small, blue blanket. Utter grief overcame Eric as his son's cries disappeared into the night.

Spots danced in front of Eric's eyes. He stared at Emily's still body. His life flickered painfully within him.

Please, let her live. Give her strength. She has to find him.

Emily took a shallow breath as Eric Wentworth's world faded to black for the final time. *I'm sorry, my love. So sorry.*

Chapter One

One Year Later

Cursing under his breath, Mitch Bradford yanked his collar up against the bitter Colorado wind. Where was Emily Wentworth going? He stalked across Colfax, on a stretch of the street known as a candy store for illicit drugs and prostitution. He could've been home alone in front of the fireplace, his bum leg propped up, nursing a stiff drink and a double dose of ibuprofen. The irony didn't amuse him. He'd been tapped for the Wentworth case *because* of his injury. One more reason to kill the guy who'd shot up his leg during his last SWAT operation.

Mitch ducked his head and plunged forward into the night, ignoring the exchange of money on the corner. He would've busted the dealer any other time, but he refused to let his suspect out of sight. When she approached a group of gangbangers, he tensed and reached for his weapon.

They circled her.

Two murders last night in the neighborhood. No time to be subtle.

He broke into a run, disregarding the twinge in his leg. He'd pay for it later, but they could shoot or stab her in seconds. Before he reached her, she tilted her head at the assailants like she was flirting and skirted through the wall of thugs. They let her go.

Mitch pulled back. Crazy woman. He tucked his Glock into the shoulder holster. He'd had enough of these cat-and-mouse games. He sped up and followed her across an alley. The scent of vomit and urine, and God knew what else, soured the night.

She stopped in front of a darkened building. After a furtive glance right, then left, she knocked. The door cracked open, then squeaked wider. Before he reached the entrance, she vanished behind the worn oak.

"Figures." Why would anything about this case be easy? Cold seeped through his jeans as he searched the front of the building for a sign. Nothing. No indication of what took place inside. That didn't bode well. His guess: drugs, sex, who knew what else.

A movement in the alley caught his attention. Carefully, he rounded the corner. A blond-haired kid tried to streak past. Mitch nabbed the boy's hoodie and lifted him off his feet. A familiar face glared at him. "Ricky?" Mitch released the young teen.

His on-again, off-again running back dusted his pants and groaned. "Coach. Man, why'd it have to be *you?* Gran'll have a fit if she has to come get me at juvie for breaking curfew."

"Then you better start talking. Is this why you haven't shown up for football practice the past two weeks? You hanging around the streets now?"

Ricky widened his stance and stared at Mitch, defiant. "I'm looking for Kayla."

"In an abandoned building?"

"Nah. Sister Kate runs a shelter out of here." Ricky bowed his head. "Kayla got herself pregnant by a real loser. But she was turning it around," he said in that earnest way that was half kid, half teenager. "At least that's what she told Gran last week. Kayla was gonna live with us again, but she didn't come back."

"You're hoping she landed here?"

Ricky nodded, and Mitch studied the street-smart kid. "You know how I can get in unnoticed?"

The boy's eyes grew large. "Something going down in there?" His gaze flickered to the front door. "Kayla might be in there."

Mitch rested his hand on Ricky's shoulder. "I don't—"

A loud, high-pitched scream pierced the night from inside. "Leave me alone. I won't go."

Ricky leaped toward the door, but Mitch held him back. He tossed the kid his cell phone. "A beat cop named Vance just rounded that corner not five minutes ago. Call 911, then get him."

"But Kayla…"

"I'll find your sister. Now go!"

Ricky took off down the street. Mitch pulled his Glock, braced, then barreled through the locked door, the rotted frame giving way much too easily. "Police," he shouted. "Nobody move."

A burly man spun around. "Do-gooders. You set me up. Well, I ain't letting 'em take me." He grabbed a pregnant girl, her face battered with yellow and green bruises, and held a knife against her throat.

"Please, Ghost. Don't do this." Emily Wentworth's husky voice shook as she stepped forward, her face pale. She clutched a bat in her hand.

She was a brave little thing, determined and fierce.

"I'm warning you," Ghost threatened.

With careful movements, she set the weapon aside. Her hand went to her throat. "Let Heather go. We'll work it out. I promise." She stepped closer.

"I said, don't move," Mitch snapped and glared at Emily. "That means everybody."

She met his gaze, the flash of fury in her eyes unmistakable, but with a curt nod backed away. Mitch took a quick survey of the room. Not a good setup. He could make the kill shot from where he stood, but he'd risk hitting the group of girls in various stages of pregnancy huddled around a nun. If Ghost had an automatic weapon under his coat, the situation could turn into a bloodbath.

Ghost pressed the knife closer, drawing blood at the girl's neck. "Back off. I'm leaving. With the girl. And you ain't stopping me."

After years on SWAT, Mitch recognized the wildness in the man's dilated eyes. "Come on, buddy. Put the knife down." Mitch lowered his weapon a bit. He could only hope the guy was high enough or stupid enough to relax his guard.

"She's coming with me. They won't pay me if I don't bring one of 'em back."

Mitch eased to his left for a better angle and met the frightened gaze of the girl. "You can't just *duck* out of here… Ghost." Mitch hunched his shoulders a bit and sagged, praying the terrified victim would understand his silent instruction.

"I don't want to go," Heather said, nodding. "I told him. Mrs. Wentworth said she'd help me." The girl went limp in the perp's arms.

Now.

Mitch spun on his good leg. One quick jab against Ghost's vulnerable back and the scumbag released his hold on the girl. Mitch shoved her toward Emily Wentworth and shifted his weight, but his injured leg spasmed and nearly buckled underneath him. He bit his cheek to block the pain as he covered the suspect with his Glock. No sirens and no telling if

Ricky had found help. Mitch needed backup before anyone realized his leg had locked up.

"On the ground. Face down. Arms spread. And you," he snapped at Emily, "call 911."

EMILY TAPPED THE PHONE to end the call. A cop. She should've known when the jerk burst through the door like some misguided superhero. He'd ruined everything. She and Sister Kate had almost guilted Ghost into talking. Now he was facedown on the floor, zip ties around his wrists, with no interest in spilling his guts to anyone. Great, just great. A month's worth of work down the drain.

Sister Kate knelt beside the man they'd hoped would be their informant. "You can tell us. It's the right thing to do."

Ghost glared at the nun. "Leave me alone."

"Sister," the cop said. "Step away from him. He's in custody."

An angry fire lit Sister Kate's eyes, one Emily had seen toast bigger brutes than this interfering officer. She waited for the blowtorch of words to fry him. In truth, she looked forward to it.

Sister Kate gave the cop a thorough once-over, then nodded her head before standing and walking away from Ghost. "You're one of the Bradford boys. Handsome as sin, the lot of you. The middle one, I'd wager. You've got the look of your daddy. I'll give you a pass. For now."

Emily almost smiled at the man's slack-jawed expression. "You know my father?"

"Oh, my, yes. Sergeant Bradford visited my halfway house to recruit for his football team. I hear you're following in his footsteps, Mitch." At his slight nod, she patted his arm. "I was sorry about what happened to him."

The man's jaw tightened, but Emily didn't miss the flash of pain across his face. She recognized the emotion all too well, but she couldn't let herself sympathize with him, even if Sister Kate was right, and his rugged good looks would make angels weep.

Emily had only one mission. Finding her son. And this cop—Mitch Bradford—had ruined her most promising lead. With nothing to lose, she bolted to Ghost and grabbed his collar. "Tell me the name," she said, her permanently husky voice still foreign to her ears, but an all-too-physical reminder of her entire purpose in life. "It's the only way you might talk your way out of this."

"Go to hell. You and your nun." Ghost flipped on his back and kicked out. A chair near his feet flew across the room. He lunged at Emily.

"Get away from him." Mitch grasped Emily's arm and yanked her to safety before subduing Ghost and pinning him with a knee to his back.

The brute on the floor grunted. "You should've stayed out of it."

"Shut up," Mitch said. He double-checked the zip-tie cuffs just as a cruiser pulled up, sirens blaring. A uniform raced inside.

"Get this guy out of here," Mitch said. "I'll file my report once I get back."

The cop nodded and escorted Ghost from the building. Officer Bradford walked toward the girls huddled in the corner, his gait slightly off when he put weight on his right leg. As he approached, they shrank away. Emily didn't blame them. It had taken her months to get past the fragmented flashes of memory when any man in a dark coat had come near her. For these teens—one girl's eye was swollen shut; another's face was mottled yellow and green from old bruises—all they'd see would be a tall, muscular brute who had shown he could incapacitate anyone who crossed him.

Then his expression softened. "You did great, Heather," he said softly. "Is everyone else okay? Anybody need a doctor?"

The girls shook their heads.

"Sister Kate takes care of us," one said, crossing her arms in defiance. "She's a nurse."

He nodded, not pushing just accepting. Emily couldn't get over the change in his demeanor. He'd transformed in seconds from a warrior—someone she was convinced could've killed Ghost if he'd wanted—to a man with a gentle gaze. Still, none of the girls would look him in the eye. His focus lowered to the discolored cheeks of one of the teens. His lips grew tight. Good. If nothing else, the evidence of abuse made him angry.

"Will you tell me about Ghost?" he said, still keeping his voice calm and low.

Amid the blare of more sirens, the girls looked as if they'd rather die than say anything.

"I got proof they're hooked up with drug dealers." Ghost's shouts rammed through the open doorway. "I can give you names, dates, places. I know their johns. I can help you put 'em away. Give their babies to people who deserve 'em."

Heather shivered and caressed her burgeoning belly. Her gaze rose to Mitch's. "He trolls for girls who get knocked up. Tries to sweet-talk the ones who haven't been around too long. He sells himself as someone who can help. We know better. They're buying a one-way ticket when they go with Ghost."

"You never see any of them again," Mitch said, the statement stark and certain, the ending unspoken.

A commotion sounded from the kicked-in doorway.

"I got something for Coach…Officer Bradford," a young kid shouted.

The cop stood and walked over to the boy, who handed over a cell phone. "I couldn't find Vance, Coach."

"That's okay, Ricky."

The boy received an affectionate ruffle to his hair, and Mitch guided the kid over to them. "Sister Kate, Mrs. Wentworth, this is Ricky Foster. He's looking for his sister, Kayla."

Over the next hour, Mitch questioned the girls and Ricky. Pregnant girls vanishing. Their babies gone. Not one of them reported missing. Until Kayla Foster.

"You'll find her?" Ricky asked, his voice laced with hope as Mitch led him to the back exit, past the front door he and Ricky had worked side-by-side to barricade to the back exit.

"Get me the picture, and I'll put the word out. We'll discover what happened."

Ricky walked out of the shelter with an expression that could only be described as cautiously optimistic.

"I wish we'd seen her." She spoke to the nun standing at her side.

"I have a feeling with Officer Bradford on the case, Ricky will be reunited with Kayla."

"It doesn't always end the way we'd want, Sister," Mitch said from behind them.

Emily hadn't realized he'd approached. She stiffened as his huge presence overwhelmed her, making her heart race. Not with fear, though. With something else—unfamiliar and enticing at the same time.

"Oh, I'm well aware of that, boy-o," Sister Kate said. "But we can't give up, can we? One soul at a time." The nun glanced at her watch. "Now, it's getting late. We're safe, and I need to do a bed check on my chickadees. Perhaps you'll walk Emily to her car? It's dark, and a pretty girl like her would do well to have a strong protector at this time of night."

The cop turned to Emily, his chocolate eyes studying her with an intensity that made her shiver. Heat rose into Emily's face, and she knew her cheeks must be crimson. When had Sister Kate turned into a matchmaker?

Her belly fluttered. He'd been so gentle and caring with the girls and Ricky, but she couldn't let herself feel anything. She just prayed a man like Mitch was watching over Joshua somewhere. And that someday she would find her son.

"You ready?" Mitch asked.

She clutched the satchel she always carried containing an age-progressed photo, fliers and the case details. Could this policeman help her? She'd never felt she could rely on the police department…or the cops in it. They'd never believed her. This man seemed different somehow, but she didn't know if she could trust him. With Ghost a lost cause, she needed another way to get information on these missing children and hopefully tie them to Joshua.

Mitch turned, and as his weight shifted to his right leg, he hesitated. She studied him for a few steps. His hip did most of the work on his right side. He tried hard not to let it show. If her job hadn't been to notice the signs of strain on the human body, he would've succeeded. He'd injured himself being a hero, trying to save them.

"You're hurt."

He stiffened, warning her to back off, but she wouldn't. Not when he was so obviously in pain. She dug into her purse for her keys and tugged out a card. "You injured yourself helping me, Officer. Come by. Let me take a look at your leg. Maybe I can do something for you." She thrust the card into his hand.

"Physical therapist, huh?"

"What've you got to lose?"

"I'm fine," he said. "Let's go."

He'd clearly shut her out. Emily remained silent, but she wouldn't forget what he'd done. He opened the back door for her, and she walked out of the haven that Sister Kate had created for her lost girls into a darkened alley filled with the sounds of angry shouts and crying babies.

When they reached the street, a tall woman in a spandex dress whistled at them. "You and your lady looking for some action?"

"No thanks. We're exclusive." Mitch tucked Emily's arm in his and shifted closer to her.

"Lucky lady," the woman said and turned her salesmanship toward a slow-moving BMW, so out of place on this street.

"You don't have to protect me," Emily said.

"After what I witnessed tonight, I'm not so sure." His gaze scanned the street before he guided her toward the crosswalk. "If you want to be a crusader, take some advice. Don't get too involved," he said. "It'll eat you up inside."

"You're a cop. You obviously think everyone's a bad guy."

Mitch's grip tightened on her arm, and he stopped. "See that kid on the corner? His name is Mario. He's twenty now. Was an amazing quarterback. Smart. Could've gone to any college he wanted. Gotten a degree. Maybe even turned pro. But he couldn't say no to his so-called friends. He was shot at seventeen. Severed the nerves in his throwing arm. No more scholarship. He gave up. He's dealing now. He'll be in prison within the year. Dead in five."

Emily doubted Mitch recognized how clearly his emotions for this young man showed on his face. "He was one of your team," Emily said. "Like Ricky."

Mitch nodded and guided her down the street. "I know the odds. I thought Mario would make it. I was wrong. I don't want to be wrong about Ricky. I'm going to fight for him. And his sister. But the odds are against them."

"You still try. And you still care."

A car screeched around the corner and barreled directly toward them. Before Emily could move, Mitch grabbed her and dove away from the oncoming vehicle. He slammed into the ground hard, wrapping her in his arms and turning so she landed on top of him. A heated gust from the car rocked them as the old Cadillac squealed past.

Mitch let out a sharp curse. "Okay, lady. Just what have you gotten yourself into?"

THE SUNSHINE-YELLOW curtains and serene green walls should've made Vanessa happy, but the colors mocked her. She'd been so very stupid. Why hadn't she left town when she'd first decided to keep her baby? The midwife had been furious. The doctor would—

A key jiggled in the lock. Vanessa huddled in the bed, cradling her newborn baby girl in her arms. Fine blond hair covered her sweet head, and Vanessa kissed the tiny cheek. "Mama will take care of you."

She prayed it would be so.

The door eased open, revealing the man who'd approach her in the mall just a few short months ago. "We had a deal." His voice was quiet and cold.

Vanessa shivered. She'd expected him to start yelling, and now wished he'd slammed open the door and screamed at her. This deadly anger made her insides quake. Bad things always happened when her daddy got like that.

"I'll pay you back. I promise." Vanessa swallowed around the lump in her throat. "I just can't give her up. I love her."

"You love her. Really? Well. That's just too bad. I have a family for her, and they aren't going to wait." He thrust a paper toward her. "Sign the form. Now."

"No."

"Marie," he called out the door. "Get in here."

The portly midwife rushed in. "But Doctor—"

"Do it."

She sighed and reached for Vanessa's baby. "I'm sorry, honey."

"You can't just take her!"

Vanessa kicked and screamed, holding on to her child, but it was no use. She was too weak from giving birth. "You can't do this," she cried as the midwife left the room with the baby. "I'll tell the police you forced me to sign. They'll give her back."

"No, my dear," the doctor said, his voice deadly soft. "You won't be telling anyone."

He moved fast, then grabbed her arm and secured one wrist with a restraint strap. She fought, rolling her body back and forth, scratching his cheek, anything to stop him.

He cursed and slapped her face. Her head snapped back, and by the time she regained her senses, he'd fastened her other hand to the rails of the hospital bed. She arched and twisted against the bindings, but he just smiled, his expression calm as he touched his hand to the cheek where she'd clawed him.

"This could've been so easy. You should've taken the money. You could've had a new life like your slutty friends," he said.

A sharp prick. She yelped at the sting as he tugged out the needle and untied her.

"What did you do to me?" She sat up, rubbed her freed hands and stared down at her arm where a small drop of blood formed.

"You'll know soon enough."

She looked at him, seeing for the first time that the eyes she'd once believed glowed with compassion were blank and hollow. "Let me have my baby. Please."

Begging him to listen, to do the right thing, suddenly she swayed. Her arms dropped, her head spun. She tried to breathe, but she couldn't. Something was choking her. She gasped. Oh, dear Lord. What was wrong? She tried to suck in air and clasped at her chest. It felt like someone was sitting on her, suffocating her. Desperately she tried to breathe, but she couldn't. The doctor's grin grew wide.

She reached out to him. "Help me. Something's...wrong."

"Sign this." He thrust the paper beneath her hand and placed a pen there. "And I'll save you."

She panted, listening to the short gasps as if she floated outside herself. She didn't have a choice. Somehow she'd get her baby girl back. But she had to stay alive.

Barely able to see the line on the page, she scrawled her name on the paper, then slumped back against the sheets. She reached out to him. "Help me. You promised."

"That I did. But then, so did you."

With the signed consent form in his hand, he walked out the door, closing it behind him.

Vanessa couldn't yell, she couldn't scream. She stared at the sunshine-yellow curtains, and they morphed into strange shapes and faces. The doctor's face. He laughed at her. Called her a fool.

And she had been. It was all her fault. What would happen to her baby?

She tried to breathe. She couldn't. Strange white spots danced in front of her eyes. There was nothing she could do. Nothing.

Please, God. Protect my baby.

Chapter Two

Mitch grimaced as he limped into the police department. What a night. And it wasn't over. He'd called in the hit-and-run. Two reports of assault in less than an hour. He'd never live it down. Especially since the busy downtown street had suddenly gone ultrasilent right after the attack. No witnesses. No nothing.

Just a woman who'd seemed quite satisfied to have been attacked. She'd met his gaze and without blinking had said, "I've got them worried. That means I'm onto something."

Unbelievable.

Half of him admired her tenacity. She scared the spit out of his other half. Come to think of it, she'd acted a lot like his late mother when he or his siblings had been on the short end of trouble. Fearless. Mitch got that. Mama-bear syndrome. Do anything for your child. But with such an overt attempt on her life, Emily'd found more trouble than she realized. She'd made someone *very* nervous.

She'd even fought leaving. Had wanted to stay, canvas the neighborhood. Only the threat of spending the night in the police station had convinced her to leave. He'd tailed her to confirm she went home and hadn't doubled back. She was safe—for now. With an unmarked unit watching her, just in case.

He glanced at his watch. Midnight was around the corner.

Finding Her Son

He was on Emily duty first thing in the morning and still had reports to file. He straightened and struggled to hide his awkward stride. At this hour, maybe he could get past the desk sergeant and the SWAT Den without seeing anyone he knew.

His thigh was on fire; his muscles were seizing up. He had less than two months to pass the physical to get his real job back. If he didn't do something drastic, he'd lose his career.

With a sigh, he sank into the hard wood of his desk chair and massaged his leg. What if he couldn't go back to SWAT? He wasn't an investigator. He didn't like analyzing and waiting. He liked breaking down doors and grabbing the bad guy. No talk. Just action. It'd felt good bringing down Ghost tonight.

"What did you do, Bradford?" Detective Dane Tanner, his temporary supervisor, stalked into the room. "You're hobbling like an old woman."

Mitch stiffened at the truth in Tanner's words. "Nothing. Just a little twinge. What are you doing here this late? I thought high-powered detectives kept banker's hours."

"Ever hear of a police radio? I keep tabs on my guys, especially those wet behind the ears like you. I heard from dispatch about your adventures tonight—you bagged this guy, Ghost, for targeting young girls. Good job." Tanner's face twisted into a scowl. "Unfortunately, he broke out of holding. A couple of street thugs created a diversion and the perp fought his way out. Put two of our guys in the hospital."

Mitch shot to his feet. "He got away? You get his prints?"

"No such luck, but we have an APB out on him." Tanner shook his head. "He's a dangerous guy. You took a big risk going in alone."

"I tried to get backup."

"Yeah, you had a fourteen-year-old kid call 911 and then try to find Vance—who'd just gone off duty, by the way.

Better men than you haven't walked away from psychos like Ghost."

"Point taken," Mitch said. His father, Paul Bradford, had been paralyzed in a shootout five years ago. Being a cop and carrying a weapon hadn't protected him. And his dad hadn't been trying to fight on an injured leg.

"I hope so. I understand investigating's not your gig. But until you pass the SWAT physical, you're stuck with us. You follow our rules. One of which is not to go in without backup. The other is not to reveal your identity to a suspect. In your case, Emily Wentworth."

"Detective—"

"Don't even try to tap dance. Lives were on the line. I get it, but you better comprehend how lucky you were." Tanner crossed his arms, staring Mitch down with a warning the ex-special forces officer clearly expected to be heeded. "Did you at least salvage the Wentworth case?"

"She noticed my leg. She offered to help me with rehab, and I've got another angle I can work to stay near her."

Mitch ran down the Kayla Foster situation, and Tanner smiled. "It sounds like you're in. We might make a detective of you after all."

"Over my dead body," Mitch growled.

"I hope not. Your dad would kill me." Tanner bent closer, his expression deadly serious. "I want this collar. Someone orchestrated Eric Wentworth's death. His murder case was stone-cold until his mother discovered that bank account in Emily's name. It's a *lot* of money and puts a whole new spin on the investigation. I want to know how the wife's involved, and I'm not backing down this time."

"If Emily's guilty, why would she offer to help me?"

"To gain an ally in the office. To get intel on what's happening in the investigation. If she arranged the hit-and-run to take out her husband, then she's willing to do anything—

including slitting her own throat—to make herself look like a victim. You and I both know that's not as uncommon as it should be."

"You're reaching. Emily almost died. Her voice will never be the same. And my neighborhood contacts don't know squat about her being involved in *anything,* except she's a do-gooder." Mitch knew he'd been mistaken in the past, but he couldn't get past his feelings about Emily. If he could trust them. "What if we're wrong? What if she's just trying to find her son?"

"Could be." His boss's jaw tightened. "But she knows *something*. And someone tried to kill her tonight. And that someone wasn't Ghost. I want an explanation." His eyes were cold. "There's dirt there. I can smell it. Find the proof. Whatever it takes."

No MORNING SUN PEEKED through the winter clouds closing in on the cemetery. The day *should* be dreary. Nothing good should happen on December fifth. Ever again. Emily ran her fingertips over the engraved inscription on the wall of stone. *Eric Wentworth. Beloved son and father.*

"Beloved husband," she whispered the words his family had denied her and wiped away a single tear.

She stood alone just inside the open archway of the Wentworth Family Mausoleum, the large marble temple as cold and unforgiving as Eric's family. They'd made their feelings perfectly clear with his marker. They had never accepted her. They blamed her for Eric's death and Joshua's kidnapping. If only she could remember that night. Something more than headlights, screams and a hooded man.

A gust of icy winter wind buffeted against her, and she stuffed her hands in her pockets. She should know what happened to her child. The diaper bag had been left in the car, but Joshua and his car seat were gone. "I still haven't found our baby, Eric," she said in the husky voice her husband wouldn't have recognized. "I'm sorry."

A lonely bell tolled from afar, and just as the tones died, a rustle of grass fluttered. She tensed. She'd had a sense all morning someone was watching her—again. For weeks she'd fought her instincts, but after last night's attack, she didn't doubt the feelings.

A looming shadow crossed the side of Emily's face. "You don't belong here."

Emily shivered at her mother-in-law's sharp words and turned slightly. Victoria Wentworth looked the perfect, elegant role of grieving mother, her black veil hiding her expression and eyes Emily knew were accusatory.

"You're not family."

"He's my husband," Emily countered softly.

"You killed him."

"Mother, you know that's not true." Victoria's son, William, stepped forward to pull her back. He shot Emily an apologetic look. "It was a tragic accident."

Victoria slapped William's hand away and faced Emily. "You set up the murder of my son and grandson. And someday I'll prove it."

Emily winced. She'd been eager to get along with Eric's family, but from the beginning the Wentworths had pushed her away until finally Eric had made a choice. He'd turned his back on them, their money and their corporation until Joshua was born and Emily had persuaded him to reconcile. Their baby deserved a family. The snowy drive to Cherry Hills Village last December had been *her* idea. In so many ways, his death in the hit-and-run truly was on her shoulders. "I loved Eric."

"You wanted a way at the Wentworth money," Victoria said as her husband, Thomas, entered the tomb and stood by her side. She reached out and clasped his hand. "Well, we won't allow it. Eric disinherited himself, and we told the insurance company his death was your fault. We even found your secret account. You'll get nothing. Nothing."

Account? "What are you talking about?"

"As if you didn't know." Victoria turned to her son. "William, get her out of here."

Victoria tilted her head into Thomas's shoulder and broke down in sobs. William whispered something to his mother and hurried to Emily.

"I think you'd better go now," he said. "I'll walk you to your car."

"I didn't *do* anything. You know that. He was my husband. I loved him." With one last look at Victoria and what might have been, Emily slid on her gloves, fighting tears of confusion, anger and hurt. William escorted her out of the cold building. Their footsteps crunched over frozen grass as they crossed toward the parking lot.

"I know you loved him," William said. "Mother can be a real witch when she wants to be. She can't let go of Eric. None of us really can."

"You think I've let go? I fight to find our son every day."

"And that's something else we have to talk about."

William's tentative voice, so similar to Eric's, sent a chill of foreboding through Emily.

"I don't quite know how to say this, so I'll just tell you. Mother and Father found my receipts for your private investigator and some of the airline tickets I bought. They came unglued when they learned I'd been helping you financially. I had to promise I'd quit."

Emily halted and faced William. "You can't stop now. I'm counting on your help." She clutched at his arm. "I'm so close."

"You've found Joshua?"

William gripped her arm, the eagerness in his voice gratifying, but she couldn't mislead him. "Not exactly. I'm collecting information on adoptions from last year because I discovered these missing babies downtown. Well, at least there are missing pregnant girls, and—"

"Oh, Emily. How many times have we traveled down this path?" He shook his head. "I'm sorry, but they're my family. In some ways they're right. It's been a year. We have to accept reality. We've tried to find him. Even my parents tried. But Joshua's gone."

"I'm not giving up. Not ever, but I need more time. With your parents painting me as a Black Widow in the gossip rags, my clinic is barely making it."

"I can't help anymore. I'm sorry." William opened the door of the decade-old compact Eric had complained about so often. When she slid onto the cracked vinyl seat, William knelt beside the car. "Take my advice. Move on with your life. Close this chapter."

"How can I do that when my son is out there somewhere? You may not believe I'll find him, but I refuse to accept that I won't."

William gripped her hands, his gaze regretful. "Then I'm sorry for you. Goodbye, Emily." He shut the door and, after a pitying look, walked back to the family crypt.

She shuddered and let out a slow breath, the cold filtering into her bones. This couldn't be happening. She started her car and cranked up the heater as high as it would go to ease her shivering, though that had little to do with the weather. She'd wondered why the life-insurance company kept stalling on the check. She had her answer. And what was that about the so-called secret account? She'd have to call the bank, but she'd never get at the money. The Wentworths would see to that.

She glanced at her watch. Officer Bradford had an appointment and would be waiting at her clinic. Could she trust him? Right now, she needed him as much as he needed her. The second phase of her plan made her stomach churn, but she had to take drastic action. She needed funds to ramp up her search for Joshua. Eric would've understood.

Snagging her purse, she dug into her pocket for the number she'd saved. With one last glance at the marble resting place of the man with whom she'd thought she'd spend the rest of her life, she placed the call. "Karen, it's Emily. Put the house up for sale. I'll take the first offer. I need the cash. Now."

THE PHYSICAL-THERAPY clinic looked too familiar. Mitch hated the fact he had a reason to enter the place, but after following Emily all morning, after zero leads on either the attempted hit-and-run, Ghost or Kayla's disappearance, the trail was subzero. He had to shake something loose.

Mitch groaned as he pushed open the door and surveyed the plethora of exercise equipment and tables. The scent of menthol wafted on the air—an odor far too familiar for his liking. Several rehab patients worked on recumbent bikes. A few more did stretching exercises with the help of staff.

When he'd discovered she had an opening this morning, he'd scrambled to get a copy of his records, threw on his sweats and headed out the door. Mitch could now infiltrate Emily's life, but he wasn't an undercover cop. He didn't like lying, he hated deceit and he was doing both. The bonus? He got the pleasure of being tortured in physical therapy for his trouble. A real win-win.

A young receptionist rounded her desk. "May I help you?"

With a quick, plastered-on grin, he scanned her name tag. "Hi, Cindy. Mitch Bradford. I have an appointment with Emily Wentworth."

The door behind them flew open, and a familiar dynamo dressed from head to foot in black raced into the room.

"Cindy, I know I'm late. Please tell me my new patient isn't—"

She skidded to a halt, clearly dismayed to see Mitch standing there. "Shoot."

Holy smokes. Emily Wentworth looked good. He didn't know how he could've missed the impact of her up close and personal last night. She was completely his type, with a petite, fit body and long, light brown hair swinging from a ponytail—obviously so silky it would be amazing spread across his pillow. Then he stared into her eyes, and his heart skipped a beat. Thick lashes framed the bluest, saddest eyes he'd ever seen. For a moment he felt lost. Her look was kind and sympathetic, with depth that could embrace his soul.

Where had that come from, waxing poetic? He had a job to do. But as he took in the plain black dress, with its high collar circling her neck, he recalled her complete aloneness at the cemetery. He'd been watching, forced to back away once the Wentworths arrived. It was the anniversary of her husband's death. Was she still in mourning, or was this all for show, all part of an elaborate plan to get at the Wentworth money?

Mitch's gut told him she was sincere. He didn't want to believe the pain on her face, the sorrow in her eyes, had been anything but real.

Then again, his gut hadn't been all that reliable lately. A few months ago, Mitch had learned his mentor had been a traitor to the badge. He wouldn't be fooled so easily now. Not anymore. He couldn't afford to give Emily the benefit of the doubt.

Mitch gave her a deliberately innocent smile. "Did I get the time wrong?"

She bit her lip, embarrassment tingeing her cheeks.

"No," she said. "I'm so sorry. Not a great way to make a first impression as a therapist. Let me change, and I'll be right with you."

"I'm not going anywhere." Not until he knew for sure whether he'd completely lost his ability to tell the good guys from the bad guys. If he was wrong about her, he'd get the evidence he needed. And if she *was* guilty, he might as well just turn in his badge.

With a smile of gratitude, she disappeared behind a staff door.

Cindy handed him a stack of paperwork. "Emily will be right back. If you'll fill out these forms…"

Mitch took the clipboard and sat in the chair closest to the receptionist before stretching his leg out. "So, I guess I was lucky to get in to see her so quickly. I heard she's really good. I thought I'd have to wait longer for an appointment."

"Oh, Emily's the best, but…" Cindy hesitated. "She's not that busy these days. Clients stopped coming because of her in-laws. They've said some things about her, and, well, some people gossip too much." Cindy bit her lip and took a furtive glance around. "I need to get back to work."

Obviously, Emily's business had taken a big hit. That money angle his boss had mentioned reared its head again, but Mitch didn't see the connection. *If* that secret account were hers, why not use it to save her business? Why work at all? Why not just disappear?

Mitch tried to get comfortable, but his leg had been giving him fits ever since that confrontation with Ghost. His body had revolted against a move he'd used a thousand times.

Once he finished the paperwork, he settled in for the long wait, but she returned in less than five minutes. Women usually took forever with clothes. Not Emily. Which shouldn't have been surprising really. Nothing had been usual when it came to this assignment. The turtleneck she wore under her scrubs was a subtle reminder of what he knew lay beneath. He'd reviewed the crime-scene photos, had seen the jagged cut across her throat that had permanently damaged her vocal cords.

"Officer, come on back." Her husky voice sent a shiver through him. He didn't know what her voice had sounded like before, but this one was downright sexy.

"Call me Mitch. If you're going to have your hands all over me, we should be on a first-name basis." He followed her into a private examining room, trying to avoid studying the sway of her hips under the scrubs she'd changed into. Down, boy. Do *not* let yourself get taken in by a pair of baby blues and luscious curves. If she were innocent and wore black on the anniversary of her husband's death, the implications made her so far off-limits, there wasn't a measurement long enough.

She shut the door and cleared her throat, nodding at the exam table. Mitch was just relieved she didn't offer to help him. His pride could only take so much. "Here's my chart, just like you requested."

He levered himself up on the table as she sat down and flipped through the pages. "You've been in therapy four months." She closed the chart. "I didn't really think you'd take me up on the offer."

"Normally I wouldn't have." The words slipped off his tongue easily—since they were the truth. "I've got two months to requalify for SWAT. I'll do anything to make that happen…Emily. Anything. And your reputation as a physical therapist… You're one of the best."

She nodded slowly. "The gunshot wound caused a lot of damage to your femoral artery and the surrounding nerves and muscles. What did your doctors say?"

"That I might never walk again. I didn't listen too hard."

A laugh escaped her, and the smile brightened her eyes. She sure was pretty.

"Good attitude. As long as you don't go too far too fast. You came a few centimeters away from losing your leg." She leaned back in her chair and set the chart aside. "Do you have the patience to follow orders? I won't work with someone who goes off on his own. Even though you saved my life. You'll need to do as I say. *Exactly* as I say."

He understood chain of command, but from this slip of a thing… He bristled and met her unyielding gaze. He couldn't afford not to play along. He'd seen the toughness in her before, the challenge. He'd give her a shot. It wasn't like he had a choice. She was his assignment. But could he get his leg strength back *and* investigate Emily at the same time? Without going crazy?

"I want my SWAT uniform back. You tell me to sweat bullets, run stadium steps, go to yoga, I'll do it. I'll even wear a Texas Longhorns jersey, and I'm an Oklahoma Sooner, born and bred. You come up with a program to help me pass that physical, and I'm with you one thousand percent."

"I'd have thought you a Colorado Buffaloes fan. But I believe you. So let's get a baseline. You wearing workout shorts under those?" She stood and indicated his sweats.

He nodded. "And just to be clear, my grandparents came from Oklahoma. Once a Sooner…"

"I get it." She smiled. "I like your loyalty to your roots, Mitch Bradford. I'll go get some equipment while you take your pants off."

A few months ago that order would have had him pulling her into his arms. Now Mitch simply slipped off his shoes, socks and sweats. He knew the drill. He'd never felt naked in a clinic before, but as he rubbed the gnarled scars on his thigh, he tensed. She'd know soon enough how damaged he really was.

After a slight knock, she entered the room. She glanced at his leg but didn't give anything away—not pity, not disgust. She moved in closer, and he caught a waft of sweet mixed with tartness. Vanilla and some kind of berry, perhaps? His heart thudded as she placed her hands on his thigh.

"Let's get started," she said.

A dozen measurements later, Mitch swiped at the sweat rolling down his face and bit his lip to stop himself from crying out. The white-hot shards of pain shooting across his thigh were much worse since his heroics of the night before. He tried to ignore them as he strained against the minuscule weight Emily had pressed against his leg. His muscles behaved like traitors. Weak as a baby.

She frowned at her notes as she compared them to his records. Then she glared at him. "What have you been doing to yourself? You've lost at least fifteen percent of your strength and flexibility gains in the past month. That didn't happen because of a single jujitsu turn. What aren't you telling me?"

Mitch grimaced, and she just shook her head. "Never mind. I know. You thought you'd be a cowboy and do a little extra on your own. More is better. Am I close?"

She shifted forward and placed her warm hands on his thigh, working the spasming muscles. Slowly, her touch eased the pain. As the agony became bearable, his focus shifted toward her fingertips on his skin, moved up her arms, to the concentration on her face. He wanted to lift her chin and lose himself in those blue eyes of hers. He wanted to forget everything that was happening around them and just escape in her caresses.

"Man, you're good," he groaned. "Can I take you home with me?" Emily on call 24/7. Part-time to massage his aching leg and part-time to take those magic hands and lips a little higher and to the left.

She worked the muscles up and down his thigh. "I know you want faster results, but if you keep working out on your own, you'll do permanent damage. You've really screwed up your leg, Mitch." She removed her hands. He missed her touch already, but her face had gone deadly serious. "I want a straight answer. Will you follow my rules?"

As he took in her no-nonsense expression, a shaft of fear sliced through him. Had he lost his chance to get back to SWAT? Follow her rules? He had no choice. For more reasons than she could comprehend. "You're the boss in the gym, Emily. I'll do whatever it takes to get the job done. I promise you that."

She paused and finally reached out her hand. "Okay. But you go off on your own, and I'm done. No second chances. Got it?"

He nodded.

The ringing cell punctuated her orders, and Emily's heart tripped at the sound. Every time she got a call, part of her leaped at the thought of good news while a small dark place trembled with fear of horrifying news. She shoved aside the terror and pulled her phone from her pocket. She glanced at the familiar number. Her pulse raced. Maybe this time… She tapped the phone and stepped away for privacy.

"Hello?" She struggled to keep her voice from being too eager, too hopeful, but she couldn't help herself.

"Mrs. Wentworth?" Her private investigator's voice crackled through the phone.

"Perry, any more on Ghost that I can use when I talk to him?"

"He lives up to his handle, ma'am. He really is a ghost, but I did get a lead. Sister Kate connected me with one of the girls. She saw a tattoo that he tried to hide. She won't go down to the police department, but she described portions of it. The art was complicated and colorful. I can fax you a picture of something similar, but I can't get into the police records, mug shots or tattoo database to verify his gang affiliation."

A tattoo. Pain shot through her temple, and she kneaded

the throbbing spot, the burn behind her eyes so familiar. A small whimper escaped her lips. It happened whenever she felt on the cusp of remembering the night of the accident. The threatening memories slipped away, and Emily pushed aside the pain.

"Another flash?" Perry asked, obviously hearing the familiar sound.

"Just images of pink, green and red."

"Like a tattoo?"

"Maybe." She let out a hiss of frustration. "I don't know. But the episodes are happening more frequently."

"You know something important, Mrs. Wentworth. You'll recall that night eventually."

She couldn't wait. She had to go to the police department. She didn't want to ask the detective in charge of her case for assistance, but wouldn't he have to listen this time? A car had tried to run her over. Ghost had threatened her. She was remembering something. "Keep digging. I'll talk to Detective Tanner." She tried to keep optimism in her voice, but even to her own ears she sounded frustrated. "Maybe he'll help this time."

Their connection ended, and she bit her lip as she studied her phone list on the small screen. A call wouldn't do any good. Tanner would only put her off again. She'd go over there and wait as long as it took to look at those tattoo records. He would give her access. She'd make sure of it.

She snagged Mitch's chart, grabbed her bag and turned to schedule the next session. He'd moved so quietly, she hadn't heard him, but there he stood, inches from her. She almost stepped on his foot and stumbled into his arms. He reached out to steady her, so close she could feel his warmth. She couldn't stop her body's reaction to his nearness.

"Whoa, there. Are you okay?" Mitch said.

Her cheeks burned hot, and she pushed back the hair that

had fallen in her face. She wanted to ask him for help but just wasn't sure enough of him. Not yet. "Sorry. I've got to run. Ten a.m. day after tomorrow okay with you?"

"I'll be here."

She bent her head to make a note, and her unruly locks fell forward again. With gentle fingers, Mitch pushed the hair back in place. His pupils went black as his gaze strayed to her lips.

She cleared her throat and stepped back, touching her fingertips to her mouth. "Um…I'd better go."

Mitch slowly nodded his head. "I think that's a good idea."

Emily filed away his record and raced out the door, her heart slamming into her chest. Her nerves tingled with awareness. Okay, so Mitch was strong and funny and determined. And hot. Despite his injury, he had a body that didn't stop.

Each step, each rub of her cotton turtleneck against her skin reminded her of what she wanted. What she hadn't experienced since before Joshua was born. Her breasts ached beneath her clothes. She couldn't deny her reaction to Mitch, but that didn't mean anything would ever happen between them. Besides, she didn't have time for a relationship. Not with anyone. Not until she found Joshua. Thinking of Mitch in any way other than a client or a potential resource was a big mistake. She was a widow. In some ways, she'd become one even before Eric had died, but her aching loneliness was *her* problem.

She looked back. He stood, watching her, his expression hooded and thoughtful. She might need him and his contacts. She'd promised to help him, otherwise she would've handed his case over to one of her colleagues. He and Carl would probably hit it off, but she couldn't risk letting go of even one potential collaborator.

She would find her son and just prayed Mitch would heal fast—before this unsettling temptation got the best of her.

THE ICY SHOWER HADN'T worked. Mitch secured the towel at his waist and padded across the cold tile of his bathroom. He'd almost kissed Emily. He'd wanted to, more so when he'd recognized the awareness that flashed in her eyes and echoed within him. He could think of a hundred reasons not to give in to the feelings, but that didn't make him want to touch her any less.

At least he'd bargained for a few hours not having to watch her. He was getting to know every curve of her body, every expression on her face. Bad news. Let another cop get tempted—until he had himself back under control.

The Oklahoma fight song sounded from his phone on the nightstand. His brother, Chase, and his best friend, Ian, gave him a hard time, but "Boomer Sooner" made Mitch grin. Who wanted Mozart or a simple ringtone? Just because his best friend and one of his siblings happened to be one pancake short of a stack and attended the University of Texas... well, sometimes you just had to live with your family's weaknesses.

"Bradford."

"It's Ian."

Mitch sank onto the bed. "Are you calling as the Coroner's Office Investigator or my goddaughter's father?"

"Sorry, bud. Haley's great, but you asked me to contact you if we received any pregnant guests. Jane Doe came in today. Not pregnant, but she gave birth just before she died. Blond hair, like the girl you asked me to watch out for."

"Is it Kayla Foster?" Mitch braced himself for the answer.

"She was in a shallow grave, so the animals—"

"Yeah. I get the picture. Was it Kayla?"

"I can't tell from the photo you sent. Her face is unrecognizable, but she has a gecko tat on her shoulder. I'm waiting on dental records."

Mitch kneaded his shoulder with his hand, working out the tension that had settled there. "How'd she die?"

"We can't tell from the external exam. Other than the birth, the body looks trauma free."

"I'd hate your job."

"At least my customers don't carry guns," Ian said.

"Funny,"

"Seriously, how's the leg?"

"Almost good as new." The lie came easily...too easily. Denial or something more after misleading Emily? "I'm a half hour away."

"See you then."

Mitch ended the call and sighed for Ricky's sake. Mitch hoped this girl wasn't Kayla. But if she wasn't, then someone else's family had a daughter who was dead, a grandchild who was missing, and they didn't know anything had happened.

By the time he reached the coroner's office, Mitch had contacted Kayla's grandmother. He'd kept the questions low-key, but he couldn't fool her.

"You bring my girl home," she'd said. "Either way."

He entered the building housing the coroner and her staff and strode down the hall to the cracker box Ian laughingly called his office. The stench of formaldehyde and death rose to greet Mitch. He hated the odor in this place. Had since he'd been forced to visit as part of driver's ed.

He rapped on the door and pushed it open to find his friend and a woman swallowed up in a white coat comparing two photos taped to a cork board. Mitch didn't give Ian's visitor a second look. He couldn't stop looking at the pictures. One the high school photo of Kayla, the other—

"Is that Kayla?" His stomach churned at the sight of what was left of a blond-haired woman's face. Truth be told, he could only tell the features were a woman because she didn't have an Adam's apple. Her eyes were missing, her nose had been gnawed away by animals. She barely looked human. He couldn't show this body to Mrs. Foster. No way. No how.

One more reason to hate his temporary assignment and get back to SWAT.

Ian grimaced and stood, blocking Mitch's view. "This is Dr. Tara O'Meare. She specializes in facial reconstruction and identification. Without dental records, I thought she could give us her opinion."

The woman rose and shook Mitch's hand.

"Is it Kayla?" he asked.

Dr. O'Meare shook her head. "No. When comparing the two photos, the distance between the zygomatic arches—the cheekbones—is wrong, and so is the position of the eyes. The girl found in the shallow grave is still a Jane Doe."

"Her grandmother said Kayla didn't have a tattoo, but I couldn't be sure."

"Grandmothers don't always know everything," Ian finished.

"Yeah. Even if the body we found isn't Kayla, I still have a missing girl out there." Mitch rubbed his eyes. A missing girl, a missing baby and a Jane Doe. Not to mention Joshua Wentworth. With Emily in the middle of it all. Which pieces fit where? He had to pull it apart section by section. Somehow. "At least for the moment, Mrs. Foster gets good news. Don't take this the wrong way, but I hope you don't call anytime soon except for a game of touch foot…" His voice trailed off.

"I'll keep calling," Ian said. "You let me know when you're up for it."

Avoiding a last look at the photos, Mitch exited the room. He tried not to breathe too deeply until he left the building, then sucked in the crisp winter air. After he inhaled several times through his nose and mouth, he could finally smell and taste the snow tumbling around him.

Once in his car, he slipped on his hands-free device and dialed Kayla's grandmother's number.

"Mitchell?" Mrs. Foster's voice trembled as she said his name.

He hated hearing the uncertainty in the woman's voice, but he couldn't guarantee the next time he called, the news wouldn't be what she dreaded to hear. "It wasn't her."

"Thank the Lord." A small prayer slipped from the older woman's lips. "You'll keep looking?"

"Definitely. I have a deal with Ricky," Mitch promised. "He shows up for practice—"

"Oh, he'll be at practice, don't you worry."

"Mrs. Foster, you know I wouldn't stop looking for Kayla, even if Ricky never—"

"I know, dear. You'll find her."

He disconnected the phone and immediately "Boomer Sooner" filtered through the car.

"Bradford."

"Get your butt down here," Dane Tanner barked. "Now."

"What's going on?"

"Your assignment just walked in the front door of the police department. Without you."

Chapter Three

"Let me see Ghost," Emily pleaded. "Or at least look through the tattoo database. It might jog my memory."

Detective Dane Tanner clicked the door closed and sat behind the interview table sporting that same patient, dubious expression Emily had grown to hate over the past seven or eight months.

"What are you doing, Mrs. Wentworth?"

"Look, Detective, I know it seems far-fetched, but I'm on the verge of remembering."

"Why Ghost? And where did this brainstorm come from so suddenly?"

Here we go again. Emily took in a slow, deep breath. "He has a tattoo."

"Did you see it? Recognize it?"

"No, but my private investigator talked to—"

"Perry Young has a spotty reputation," Tanner said. "I've reiterated this every time you've brought one of his leads to me. All going nowhere, I have to remind you. He's a gambler and a drinker." The detective shuffled through some papers. "He's stringing you along for a steady paycheck."

Not so steady anymore. That's why she had to convince the detective to help her now.

"I got a flash of memory, Detective. If I could just see Ghost's tattoo, or at least look at the books, I might recognize something. Ghost's in custody, right? How tough would it be for me to talk to him?"

"I'm not breaking protocol because you had a *vision*. Go to a tattoo parlor."

"I know what you think of me, Detective Tanner, but do it for the missing girls. Maybe Joshua and their babies are connected."

"No infants have been reported missing or stolen. I'm sorry." Dane steepled his fingers and rested them against his lips.

"A pregnant girl is missing."

"And Kayla Foster's grandmother reported her. This MO's not a fit for Joshua's disappearance. It's none of your concern."

She launched out of her chair and leaned over the desk. "You can't turn your back on the vulnerable. Joshua is only thirteen months old. He's alone." She hated the idea of begging—especially to the detective who didn't trust her—but she'd do anything for her son. She knew the statistics, the chances of getting him back. Infants taken who weren't returned within a few weeks were almost never found. The numbers didn't matter. Joshua would be the exception. She grabbed the age-progressed photo from her satchel and shoved it at him. "Please. Ghost tried to force Heather to go with him. You have to help those girls. I can help, too, if you'll let me."

"I'll pass the information to the officer in charge of the assault case. That's the best I can do. You, however, couldn't have come in at a better time." The detective slid a document across the table. "Is that your signature?"

Emily stuffed the photo back into her bag, scanned the paper and lifted her chin. "You want to quiz me about money or bank forms, call my lawyer. My son is out there, and I need help to find him. If you won't do it, I'll find someone who will."

She slammed out of the interrogation room, the wooden door banging behind her, and sagged against the wall. Her heart pounded as reality set in. The Wentworths had closed nearly every door. She'd have to scrape together enough money for an attorney and for Perry. God help her if they blocked the sale of the house somehow.

"Emily?"

The deep voice that she shouldn't have recognized so easily sent a flood of hope through her. "Mitch." She turned, then rushed over to him. "What are you doing *here?* I thought you were SWAT."

"Temporary assignment while I'm rehabbing." He clasped her arm and guided her toward a chair next to a desk with his name. "What's going on?"

Mitch's concern wrapped around her like a warm blanket. She looked up as he escorted her, strong and able—almost a knight in shining armor. Last night, even though someone had almost killed her, she'd felt safe and protected in his arms after he'd snatched her out of harm's way. Could she trust him to do the same now?

She had no choice. She had to go with her instincts. She sat down and clutched her evidence satchel meeting his gaze. "Detective Tanner."

"My temporary boss," Mitch clarified gently as he hitched his hip on the edge of the desk.

"Oh." Maybe this hadn't been such a good idea, but she'd run out of options, and no matter what William had advised, she wasn't giving up. "I received a tip about Ghost's tattoo, and it reminded me of something from the night of the accident. I asked Tanner to let me see the mug shots or the tattoo database, but he won't. He wouldn't even let me see Ghost."

"Did you see his tat?"

"Well, no, but I heard one of the girls—"

"Tanner's a real by-the-book kind of guy," Mitch said. "He doesn't bend regs. If you didn't see the tat, he won't let you at the photos."

"Do *you* ever break the rules?"

Mitch quirked a small smile. "Let's just say in SWAT sometimes a little creative thinking is required. I wouldn't say I break regulations, but I might bend them a bit."

Hope flickered through Emily as she stared at the man who had taken down Ghost. She leaned forward in her chair and gripped Mitch's arm. "I need your help to find my son."

"I'm not a real investigator, Emily. Just on temporary assignment. You need—"

"I need someone who believes in getting at the truth…and in finding Joshua. No one here does. They never have." Bitterness crept into Emily's voice. "I know you've heard the rumors, but they're not true. I loved Eric. Please, help me find Joshua."

She saw the turmoil and indecision in his eyes, and something that almost looked like guilt. "It's not your fault this department has let me down, but you can change that."

"Bradford. In my office. Now."

Tanner's order made Emily jump, but Mitch had been expecting the interruption. He patted her arm. "I'll be right back. Don't worry."

He walked into his boss's office.

"Wentworth came to see me like you said she would. So… what does she want from you?" Tanner asked.

"Help to find her son. Because she doesn't trust the rest of your unit."

The detective sank back into his chair and smiled. "This couldn't be better if I'd planned it. Do it."

"Tanner—"

"This is your chance. She might let something slip. Maybe

her son's disappearance was part of a plan gone wrong. But even if she's not involved, she knows something. Tell her you talked me into letting you take over her investigation. Tell her you need to stick close because of Ghost's escape. Earn her trust."

"But—"

"Get out there before our chicken panics and runs away. Work Emily any way you can. Find out if she's into something that got her husband killed and her son taken. I'll work the money angle. I want to know who murdered Eric Wentworth."

His boss's jaw twitched as he passed over a single cardboard box. "Here are copies of the key forensic and evidence reports on the accident and kidnapping. No real leads. Most of that file's full of initial interviews and her PI's false tips. It's been vetted. Show it to Wentworth. Use it to gain her trust and get her reaction."

"I'll do my best." Mitch snagged the evidence and stared at his boss. "Why so rabid on this, Tanner?"

His boss let out a long sigh. "Eric Wentworth called me the day before he died. I'd taken time off. Turned off my cell. Wentworth said he had some vital information for me, but he needed to be discreet. No details on the message. He died before I could return the call. I never turn off my phone anymore."

"Damn, Dane."

"Find out who killed him."

Mitch gave a stiff nod to his boss and pasted a satisfied expression on his face as he returned to the bullpen. He lifted the box. "It took some convincing, but I got the case."

Emily's face broke into a relieved smile. Guilt burned through Mitch's gut. He liked straightforward and honest, not games.

He shifted the evidence in his arms. "Look, we *should*

talk in the conference room, but let's get out of here first. It may be bending the rules a bit, but there are things I need to tell you, and—" he peered around the room "—we have an audience."

Emily looked about then turned to Mitch. "I've been watched more than enough in this police station. Follow me to my place. Let me show you what I've done. Maybe you'll see something I haven't." She snagged a sticky note and pen from the top of his desk and scribbled her address. She handed him the yellow paper. "Just in case I lose you."

He took the slip but didn't need the information. He'd memorized her address.

Mitch didn't like the sour taste success left in his mouth. Emily trusted him, and every word he spoke had a lie hidden behind it. He'd have to live with the consequences.

As they passed the desk sergeant, one of his SWAT-mates, Reynolds, ran past. "Mitch. Wish you were back, man. We got a bad one at the Denver Federal Center."

Reynolds shoved through the doors to the SWAT Den, and Mitch could see the flurry of activity.

"Okay, children. Mount up," Lieutenant Decker, his SWAT commander, yelled.

The steel door closed out the noise. Mitch's knuckles whitened around the box handles. "I should be there." But until Ghost was caught, he couldn't let this case go…whether he was reinstated to SWAT or not. Emily was in danger, and he couldn't turn his back on his responsibility to her.

He felt the warmth of her hand on his arm.

"You'll get back to them," she said. "Soon."

Was her concern real or had she recognized his desperation to return to SWAT? Was Tanner right? Was she a black widow? A beautiful, tempting black widow, but a dangerous predator nonetheless?

God, he hoped not. They walked out together.

After shoving the box in his SUV, Mitch followed her around winding curves to an isolated neighborhood that backed up against the Rocky Mountains. She slowed to fifteen miles below the speed limit when they reached the curve where the accident had occurred. A single white cross with a red wreath of poinsettias decorated the side of the road. He'd watched as she placed them there. Would she stop as she sometimes did?

After slowly passing the spot, she sped up and took a few more turns to her house. A picket fence surrounded her ranch-style home. As she pulled into the driveway, Mitch frowned at the Priced to Sell sign in the front yard. That was new since this morning. So, money was as tight as Tanner believed.

He grabbed the evidence box from the backseat and met her at the front door. "How long has it been on the market?"

"Not long."

"You're in a nice neighborhood. That should help it sell faster."

"I hope so," Emily said. "Let's go into the dining room."

They passed a kitchen, and Mitch noted a single cereal bowl and coffee cup on a drying towel. Nothing out of place. He glanced past a living room with a layer of dust on most of the wood surfaces. He hadn't expected that. No magazines, no DVDs thrown about. The house didn't really look lived in. He opened his mouth to pry as she slid open a walnut door. The words stuck in his throat when he entered the dining room.

"Whoa." The walls had been converted to murder boards. Articles, photographs, dates had been attached, connected with arrows and lines, and adorned with notes.

Emily pointed to one side. "It's a timeline of every event from the month before the hit-and-run until one month after.

On the map, I've recorded every infant kidnapping in North America."

Mitch rounded the dining room table and stepped up to the dozens of photographs tacked across the country. "You have *found* written on all of them. None of these kids are still missing."

"Except Joshua."

"And the small *d* in the corner of the photo?"

"Deceased," she whispered.

Her words had gone so soft he could barely hear her. She probably hadn't been able to write the word. Either way, the letter became a stark reminder of the worst that could happen.

He studied the third side of the room. Tips and newspaper clippings of missing children papered from ceiling to floor. On the final wall, a photo of Sister Kate's refuge. She'd added two large questions. *How many babies? Adoption?*

No wonder what he'd seen of the rest of the house looked untouched. She spent all her time in this room, searching for clues to her son's whereabouts. He couldn't get over the detail. He disliked the tediousness of investigation, and this amazing woman had taught herself most of the techniques they'd covered in Mitch's training at the police academy. She impressed him more and more with each passing moment.

"You've done a lot of work."

"Not much else to do." She sat in one of the hard cherry chairs, the only one that wasn't perfectly aligned around the table.

"You have any help?"

"No one else seems inclined. Including your boss."

Mitch didn't blame her for the accusation in her tone. "What about your friends, family?"

"My brother's stationed overseas. And friends… It's been a while since I had any of those."

Mitch let his surprise show. "You seem like a person people would latch onto—for movies, hiking, dinner."

"I make most of my old friends...uncomfortable."

She brought a self-conscious hand to her throat. Mitch had become accustomed to her husky voice, in fact he liked it, but it was another reminder. "Because of your son."

"And this room. They said I was obsessed...the few who came over." She clasped a locket resting on the outside of her turtleneck. "I remind them that nightmares can happen. Do happen."

"You won't give up until you find him."

"Never. No matter what the Wentworths say or do."

Mitch eyed a high chair pushed into the corner, a bib draped over the back. A small teddy bear with one blue eye and one brown eye sat in the seat right next to an empty wooden cradle. Unused for the past year. She faced the memory every day. This woman didn't know where her child was. She didn't know who took him. If she'd had anything to do with her husband's death, she would know where to start.

If she were playing him, if this were an elaborate hoax, she deserved an Oscar. His job was to prove one theory or the other.

Placing the box with the few flimsy files on the floor, he sat beside her and stretched out his leg. "Let's ignore the records for now and start from the beginning. What do you remember about that day?"

Emily's expression fell, her vulnerability embedded in her eyes. Then she straightened her shoulders with an inner strength he recognized even after only a few conversations. While part of him wanted to take her into his arms and comfort her, he couldn't. He'd already crossed a line. He liked her. He believed her. He had to keep his distance. No matter how tempting he found her.

"I try to remember the details of that night a dozen times

a day," she said. "I don't know exactly what happened. Everything seemed fine. We'd barely left the house on the way to Eric's parents'. The road was slick, but nothing out of the ordinary. I remember the lights coming at us, and flashes, the sound of Joshua's cry—" her husky voice caught "—a hooded figure, but not much else."

She rubbed her eyes with one hand and clutched at her throat with the other. "By the time I regained consciousness, a week had passed. Eric was dead. His family had held the funeral, and they blamed me for his death and Joshua's disappearance. More than that, they thought I had something to do with the crash." She reached out a hand to Mitch. "I know they believe I cut myself with the glass, but I would never… You have to believe me."

"Think, Emily," he said. "We know from the paint scrapes that you and Eric were run off the road. The question is why. They took your baby. Was your son the target? Had you been threatened?"

She shook her head firmly. "Nothing like that. Look at the map. Infants aren't taken very often, not by strangers. And most of the time they're found within two weeks. There's not a slew of stolen babies in any one geographical area. Not anywhere in the country. And certainly not here."

Mitch rose and turned to the map. He ran his finger from pin to pin. "I know that. I don't necessarily think your son was taken as part of a baby ring. This was personal. About your family." He faced her. "You and your husband took out a life-insurance policy just before he died. Why?"

Emily stilled, her entire body tense with suspicion. "Wait a minute. How do you know about the insurance? And the paint? I just asked for your help today."

Oh, boy. His first big slip. Well, one thing SWAT had taught him was to think on his feet. "Tanner mentioned a few things, but I have to admit, after last night, I looked into your case. I didn't think the attempted hit-and-run was an accident. I still don't."

How long could he mix truth with lies and still remain credible? The question churned in Mitch's gut.

"Ghost could've called someone. He threatened me. Did you ask him?"

Mitch let out a long, slow breath. "I've got some bad news about Ghost. He's no longer in custody."

"You let him go?" She rose from her seat, her eyes sparking with fury. "How could he make bail? He'll disappear." She crossed to Mitch, hands planted on her hips, toe-to-toe with him.

He hated to admit the truth. "That's not quite what happened. He escaped. Before we could get prints or mug shots."

"I *have* to talk to him." Emily paced around the room. "He's all I've got."

"You can't, Emily. That's one reason Tanner gave me your case. I believe, and he agrees, that you're in danger. He knew, given your history with the police department, you wouldn't be receptive to protection."

"He was right about that." Emily glared at him. "Your boss should've told me the second I asked to see Ghost. He lied to me. And so did you."

"We didn't tell you everything," Mitch acknowledged.

"How am I supposed to trust you? I thought you were on my side. That you believed me."

"I do believe you. I don't think you know where your son is, but Ghost threatened you, and I'm sure he'll come after you. You need my help."

Emily let out a slow breath and met his gaze. "If we're going to work together, you can't lie to me, Mitch. Or keep secrets. I can't do that again." She bit her lip and turned away.

"Wait a minute." Mitch touched her shoulder. "What do you mean *again?*"

She whirled around and raised her chin in challenge. "It doesn't matter. You want to know about the money. Eric and I bought the policy because of the baby. Joshua was only a month old, but Eric planned for the future, especially since he and his family…weren't communicating."

Mitch didn't like the frozen expression on Emily's face. He'd really blown it. "Your husband didn't get along with his parents?"

"They'd been estranged for a while. Ever since, well, ever since we got engaged. I wasn't quite the daughter-in-law they had in mind. Not blue-blooded enough, if you get my meaning. They made no secret of it, so Eric left the family business. He gave up everything for me."

"Their loss," Mitch said before he could help himself.

Emily looked at him, her expression full of sadness. "It's easier to think I arranged this entire thing than acknowledge someone could have stolen Joshua and he's still out there."

"You believe he's alive."

"I have to." She lightly touched the photo of her son pinned to the wall, her eyes glistening. "Do you understand that?"

"More than some." He turned her to him and, with a gentle tug, pulled her closer. "I don't have kids, but I have a goddaughter. Her mother took Haley out of the country and wasn't planning on returning her to her father. I helped find her and bring her home."

"Is she…okay?"

"Oh, she's more than back to her old self." He couldn't help but smile at the thought of the shenanigans of his favorite and only goddaughter. "She'll turn six soon and has her daddy wrapped around her little finger."

"Maybe that will be me someday." A shuddering sigh escaped from Emily.

Haley's story had done more than sympathizing with Emily could ever do. The ice in her eyes had softened.

"I'll do my best to help you find your son," he said truthfully. "I promise that."

Emily reached out and laid her hand over his heart. "I believe you."

The utter faith in her words humbled him. Unable to resist, he cupped her cheek, and she tilted her head into his hand as if searching for warmth, for comfort, for something to hold on to. His heart slammed against his chest. His gaze lowered to her lips. Her tongue moistened them, and her eyes deepened to a rich cobalt. The awareness between them surged. Mitch knew it was wrong, but he wanted to comfort her. He wanted her to know she wasn't alone.

He leaned in and let his hand roam down her cheek to the edge of her turtleneck. Her pulse jumped beneath his fingertips. He stroked her palm with soft, tender caresses. She shivered, and her body moved in closer. The heat emanating from her made Mitch long to feel her softness pressed against his chest.

His fingertips drifted up her arms. Very gently he brought her to him. With a soft groan he lowered his head slightly. Her lips parted, her eyes drifted closed.

She sucked in a quick breath. "No. I can't."

He clasped her hands in his and studied their entwined fingers. If only he'd met Emily at another time, another place. When he could let himself get lost in her arms. She might've been the woman he could've trusted to fall asleep with and never worry about betrayal. "I understand." With regret— and relief—he eased away. "I'm sorry."

"Don't apologize. Everything's just confusing right now."

Mitch stood and turned away, willing his body to calm down. "Let's get back to work." He lifted the lid off the cardboard box of evidence. The photo on top was of a smiling blond-haired man and a radiant Emily on their wedding day. No sadness in her eyes, only joy.

He wanted Emily, but he shouldn't get involved. He couldn't let himself care too much. Not when everything he said was a lie. When she found out why he was really here, helping her, but spying on her at the same time, she'd never forgive him. God knew he'd never forgive himself.

"Let's go through the evidence box and compare it to your data," Mitch said to distract his traitorous body. He placed the box on the table. "Maybe something in these interviews will jog your memory."

Emily peered inside, and her hand paused over the wedding photo. "We were happy. Everything was perfect."

Or was it? Those last few weeks, Eric had pulled away. He'd said it was work and soon everything would be fine. He'd kept his secrets, and then she'd lost him.

His laughing eyes captured her. What would he think of her now? A year after his death, letting herself get taken in by the first cop who'd shown her any sympathy. She'd almost let Mitch kiss her, but he wasn't being her friend. Not really. How long would he help? Until Tanner pulled him into a more important case?

Her cell rang, and she answered.

"I need to see you," Perry said. The PI's voice was quiet. "I have a lead on your son. It's big, Mrs. Wentworth. *Really* big."

"The police department—"

"No. No cops. Can't trust anyone. Especially not the law. I don't know who's looking the other way there, but someone is."

"You're saying someone at the police department is involved?"

Mitch's head snapped up. She backed away, and he nearly dove for her. He pried the phone from her and, before she could protest, pressed the speakerphone button.

Emily shook her head vehemently and tried to grab the device.

"Do you trust me?" Mitch mouthed.

Did she trust him? His intense gaze made her insides quiver. His every action made her believe he wanted justice. The way things were going right now, she had to take a chance. She nodded, and he handed her the phone.

"You there, Mrs. Wentworth?"

"Sorry, Perry. Um…where do you want to meet?"

"I'm on my way back to Denver. Be at the main library when it opens in the morning."

Mitch scribbled a note on a piece of paper and passed it to her.

Must have proof.

"I'll be there, but I need something concrete, Perry."

"You'll have more than that, ma'am. I'm gonna find your kid."

With a shaking hand, Emily ended the call. "You've got a lot of nerve."

"My rules when it comes to the investigation."

"Perry's not the kidnapper. I don't like deceiving him."

"You need more than Perry. No offense, Emily, but he's not exactly top drawer. Word on the street is he has a drinking problem."

"Well, if I don't sell this house soon, I won't even have him. You're going to be my only resource." The stark truth made the long journey seem bleak, with only bright memories of Joshua lighting the way.

"Then let's get back to the evidence," Mitch muttered.

Darkness had long since cloaked the house when they came up for air. Emily's vision had gone bleary despite the pots of coffee and snacks they'd consumed. She glanced at her watch and blinked. "It's getting late."

"I'm not going anywhere," Mitch said, his voice flat and no-nonsense. "Not with Ghost at large."

"You're not thinking of staying here tonight." Or maybe he was. She studied the man who'd spread out at her dining-room table, surrounded by snacks, pens, stickies and a note-pad.

"Nonnegotiable," he said, pulling out another file. "I've got coffee, work, a laptop, the internet, my gun and a beautiful damsel in distress. What more could a guy ask for?"

Stunned, Emily sat back in her chair, studying the determined face of the man who'd suddenly turned into her champion. "Why are you doing this?"

Mitch walked over to the empty cradle and lifted the teddy bear with a gentle hand. "You've been doing this on your own long enough," he said. He centered the bear on the table. "And I don't like unanswered questions. Besides, sleep is over-rated."

"It's been a while since I've done an all-nighter," she said. "But I'm game." She took a sip of coffee and settled in for the duration.

MORNING CAME TOO QUICKLY. They'd barely moved. "What are we doing?" Emily said tossing another stack of notes to the table, her voice cracking. "There's nothing here. That's why I hooked up with Sister Kate. Desperation. Missing babies. Except they aren't missing. Detective Tanner was right. There's no connection."

"Not yet. Did you expect me to pull out a miracle in one day?"

"You're so determined, maybe I hoped you would."

She studied his alert expression and half smile. After a night together, she'd become ultra-aware of Mitch's sense of humor, his addiction to sugar in his coffee and his need to stretch his leg every few hours. He never complained, of course. She also appreciated his keen wit and how quickly he leaped from fact to fact, even though most led to dead ends. Sitting next to him, passing papers back and forth, touching casually a thousand different ways, made Emily feel more comfortable with him. It felt good. To have a real partner again.

She knocked shoulders with him, but when she should have pulled away, she lingered, giving in to a desire that had simmered the entire night. Their hands touched before she drew hers away, her face heating. "Sorry."

"Don't be." Their gazes caught, his lowering to linger on her lips.

He let out a long, slow breath. "Time to meet Perry. I'll follow you."

"He won't like it."

"I don't much care what he likes. If he has evidence against the department, I want to know about it."

Mitch packed up the evidence box and loaded in some of Eric's bank statements. Emily grabbed her purse and evidence satchel and, with a last glance at the murder boards, said a small prayer. Once outside, she slipped into her car and pulled out of the driveway with Mitch tailing her.

When she and Eric had moved into the house, she'd loved the view of the pine trees along the serpentine curve. Even the steep drops on either side of the road hadn't fazed her… not until that night a year ago.

She navigated the car along the narrow stretch of asphalt. A metal sign loomed toward her on the left. Her heart always jumped a bit as she approached the turn. Some days were worse than others, but she handled it. Once she found Joshua she'd conquer the road forever.

The gleaming white of the cross loomed at the horizon. She waited for the splash of poinsettias to come into view, but the flowers were gone.

Oh, God.

A small blue blanket splattered in red was draped over the top of the white cross.

Pain exploded behind her eye, throbbing in her head. Blood. Everywhere. Images, sounds. Joshua's cry. A flashlight. Eric's gray face. Blood pulsing from his chest. Red and green. Pain. Pink. Blood. Blue blanket.

Joshua. No! The blanket wasn't his. It couldn't be.

She had to stop. She had to know. Heart racing, she panted. She couldn't breathe. Her foot slammed into the floor. The car didn't slow down.

Her knuckles whitened on the steering wheel. A burning hit her throat. The copper taste of blood exploded in her mouth and lights flashed in her eyes.

She pumped the brake. Nothing.

The car sped faster on the downward incline. The metal guardrail raced past her. This couldn't be happening. She gripped the steering wheel so hard her hands cramped, and she kept pounding the pedal, but it was no use.

The slight slope became steeper. Fifty miles per hour. Fifty-five.

A hairpin curve waited ahead. She'd driven the road countless times, but not this fast. Never this fast.

Snow began to fall, small flakes.

Not again.

Behind her a loud honking sounded, but she couldn't afford to look in her rearview mirror. The phone in her pocket rang, but she couldn't pick up. She struggled to keep the car on the road. Much more snow and the road would become too slick. She'd never make the curve.

With all her strength, she wrenched up on the emergency brake.

Nothing.

Please, Mitch. Help me.

The road seemed to narrow; the cliffs on either side seemed to go on forever. Her life couldn't end here. Not in this place. Not before she found Joshua.

A car sped past her. Mitch.

"No brakes!" she screamed, as though he could hear her.

Mitch's SUV raced in front of her. He slowed down, and her car shoved into his rear bumper. They rounded the curve, but she was going too fast.

Emily struggled to steer. Her tires hit black ice. She skidded toward the cliff.

Joshua, I won't die. I promise.

Chapter Four

"No!"

Mitch watched in horror as Emily's compact car spun out of control. He had to save her. He wrenched his steering wheel and maneuvered his vehicle between her and the guardrail, pumping his brakes. Her vehicle shoved into his driver's side door.

With a curse, he turned into the spin, until finally his four-wheel drive caught traction. Tires squealed, and he gauged the distance to the edge. It was going to be close.

"Come on, baby. Stop." He yanked on the emergency brake, spun the steering wheel hard to the left and prayed. Brakes sparked and metal ground against metal as they skidded toward the drop-off.

The spin slowed the momentum, but the mountain's edge came barreling at them. Mitch's arms shook under the strain of turning the fused metal coffins, but it was working. They were slowing. Three feet away. Two feet away. Inches away, and finally, the front ends of both vehicles shuddered to a stop. A waterfall of rocks plunged hundreds of feet down.

He forced open his smashed door and headed toward Emily. Her driver's side had melded to his SUV; her head lay against the window. He rounded to the passenger side. He squeezed, then jiggled the handle, but it was jammed.

"Emily. Can you hear me?" He pounded on the glass, ignoring the icy wind that whistled up from the canyon and the sky threatening to turn into a storm.

She didn't move. No air bag on this ancient tin can.

She was so still. Too still. He had to get to her.

He ran his fingertips alongside the crumpled metal, searching for a seam. Yes, right there. He snagged a crowbar from his SUV. If he could get the leverage... He inserted the iron rod and, using his body weight, worked against the hinge. The metal finally gave way, and he forced open the door.

He dove into the car, careful not to jostle her too much. With a gentle touch, he moved some silky strands away from her face. No obvious wounds that he could see. He leaned closer.

"Emily?"

She groaned. At the sound, relief released terror's grip on his heart. "Can you move?"

Those ridiculously long lashes blinked, and her eyes focused on him. "What happened?"

"Brakes."

She nodded, and then her expression took a leap from confused to horrified. "The blanket!" She pulled at the door handle and looked at the crumpled side of his vehicle outside her window.

"It was the only way to stop you," he said, unclicking her seat belt. "Slide toward me, but let me know if anything hurts. Your car jammed into mine pretty hard."

She eased toward him, pausing as she tested one limb, then the next. "I'm okay. Just shaken."

As he clasped her hands, a distinctive odor slammed his senses. Gasoline.

No time to waste. He yanked her away from the car. "Move!" he yelled, grabbing her hand and hauling her toward a large boulder.

She stumbled after him, but her legs gave way. She sagged

to the ground. He swept her into his arms. Within seconds, he reached the large rock and settled her behind the massive boulder.

"What do you think you're doing?" She glared at him. "Your leg can't handle my weight."

"That'll be the day, when I can't carry a little thing like you. As to why—gas. Would you rather risk a spark setting your car on fire?"

"It doesn't sound like anything's happening." She tilted her head toward him. "Maybe we—"

His ears picked up a clicking sound over the wind. He held up his hand, and she went quiet. Mechanical. Definitely.

And familiar.

"Get down." Mitch shoved her to the dirt. A loud explosion shook the ground. Flaming debris flew toward them, hot metal and plastic shrapnel. Mitch covered her body with his, shielding her from the incoming.

Several hot projectiles nipped his back. He brushed them away. Soon the mini-explosions had stopped and only the roar of fire remained. He raised his head and scanned the wreckage. From their vantage, he could see fire leaping between the vehicles, taking out his SUV and charring what was left of Emily's. The remains might have been her grave.

The thought that she could've been pinned in the death trap froze his insides, but the fury at the psycho who'd planted the bomb boiled his temper. Emily could've died. On his watch.

He grabbed his phone and pressed a key. "This is Mitch Bradford. Get me the fire department and bomb squad. Now."

Mitch rattled off their location and ended the call.

"A bomb?" she said, her voice huskier than usual. "I thought the car exploded because of the accident."

"That's Hollywood. I heard suspicious clicking right before the explosion. There was at least one device, maybe more. Someone wants you dead—with no evidence left behind."

"If you hadn't been here…"

She gripped his shirt and buried her head against him. He'd seen the reaction before. Violence wasn't pretty, and the human spirit needed comfort.

He held her tight. "We'll find out who's doing this. I promise."

She wrapped her arms around his neck and hugged him tightly. He couldn't say no to her trembling frame. Each shudder evoked every protective instinct throbbing in his veins. He cradled her against him and stroked her head softly, brushing a few stray snowflakes out of her hair. "You're okay. It'll be okay."

He was lying. Again. This assassin wanted a kill. Mitch could only stop him so long—unless he discovered who was behind the attempts on her life.

Emily lifted her hand to his face, and her look of trust made his heart do a crazy flip-flop. "I'm only here because you saved me. I would have gone over the edge, and Joshua—" Emily's eyes widened. She gripped Mitch's arms hard, her nails biting into his flesh. "Joshua. The blanket! The blood. I have to check the blanket and see if it's Joshua's."

She rose, swaying as the heat from the fire buffeted them. Emily tugged at his hand in desperation. Mitch shifted his weight to his good leg and pulled her back. "Emily. Listen to me. We are *not* going out in the open. We're safe here."

"I have to see that blanket."

"No. The person who sabotaged your car could be waiting. You're not stepping into someone's crosshairs."

Mitch went to wrap his arms around her, but she shoved him back. Any vulnerability she'd let him see had vanished.

"I'm *already* a target." She pulled at her turtleneck and revealed the jagged scar on her throat. "The doctors said I held the glass. That I cut myself. Well, I didn't. And no one believes me, because my prints were on the shards." She met his gaze. "I put flowers on that cross just yesterday. I *have* to see that blanket. I have to know if there was…blood there. I need to know I'm not imagining things."

"I saw it, Emily. You're not crazy. Stay with me."

"I can't. I need to know." She jerked out of his arms and took off up the mountain. Mitch cursed, drew his weapon and started after her, his mind whirling. Emily's scar was vicious. She'd almost died. Had that been the perp's first mistake? If Emily had died from the wound, the whole hit-and-run could very well have been classified murder-suicide gone wrong.

The perfect crime. Her son would've been presumed dead.

She ran up the hill. She was in good shape. Normally Mitch would've caught her in a few steps, but his strides were uneven these days. He was gaining on her, but not fast enough. Mitch's eyes scanned the surrounding terrain. On one side of the road, the cliff was steep. Not impossible to hide there, but tough. The other side made them vulnerable.

Finally, he caught up with her. She'd stopped, bent over, trying to catch her breath. Her swaying made him curse again. "You're pushing too hard. You could be hurt and not know it."

"I'm not stopping until I get that blanket." She sucked in a lungful of air. "You wanted evidence. That's evidence."

"I should tie you up, but I can see it won't do any good." As frustrating as he found her determination, he admired it. "When we get there, don't touch anything. And stay on my right. Between me and the steep side."

Together they rounded the last curve. The cross poked out of the ground—a wreath of plastic poinsettias draped around it, a light dusting of snow completing a hideously wrong yet serene picture.

No blanket.

"What?" Mitch had seen the blanket and the red splatter pattern.

Emily collapsed on the side of the road. "They're trying to drive me crazy."

"You're not crazy." Mitch pulled her to her feet and lifted her chin. "Whoever's doing this is vicious. They used the blanket to make you hit your brakes. It was a setup. They tried to kill you and make it look like an accident, but they failed. You didn't go over the side of the road. You're here."

"But the blood?"

"It wasn't real. Too bright. Dried blood is dark in color."

She sagged against Mitch. "Joshua has to be alive. I can't go on if he isn't."

"We'll find Joshua. I promise." It was a vow he would probably regret making, but right now, at this moment in time, it was the right thing to do.

He scanned the area. Just to the side of a recently replaced guardrail, several tall pines and an outcropping of boulders would be good cover—at least until the units showed up. Mitch lifted her in his arms and walked to the shelter. Such a tiny thing. He set her down and unzipped his coat, tucking her against his chest, and held her.

He stood there, holding her, their body heat combining, the outside cold seeping away as he surveyed the landscape surrounding them, searching for a sign, a movement, of anyone watching them. A slight shiver fluttered through Emily.

"Why are they doing this to me?"

Her quiet voice twisted Mitch's heart. He'd seen enough depravity in his time at SWAT to realize human beings could do almost anything, but what they'd done to Emily took true desperation…and a special kind of callousness.

"I'm going to find out," he said.

She shifted away from him and pushed her hair out of her face. "I need to call Perry. He'll worry." She reached into the pocket of her jacket and pulled out the phone. Not much charge, but she pressed the button. "It still works."

Mitch stayed her fingers. "Perry knew when you were going to rendezvous. You realize that."

"I could've been anywhere when he called. He didn't know I was home."

"Not unless he's been following you," Mitch said. "You have to consider he's been paid off. His history—"

"I don't want to believe that. Except for William, he's the only one who ever helped me."

Mitch wanted to shout, "Until me," but he couldn't. The words were almost true. How could investigating her and deceiving her be considered helping her? No. Too many lies lay between them. He couldn't add one more. Trouble was, she was getting to him.

Screaming sirens tore up the mountain. Mitch's focus shifted from Emily to the decorated cross to her cell phone. He couldn't be sure who to trust, either. This case had just become very complicated.

EMILY SAT IN A PATROL car, out of the freezing wind, as law enforcement crawled all over the mountain like a swarm of ants. Quite the response when a SWAT officer's personal vehicle blew up. They'd blocked off the road and now searched for evidence.

The stench of burning rubber and plastic filled the air. The odor made her stomach roil, though not as much as the thought of what someone was willing to do to get her out of the way. All she wanted was to find Joshua. Why couldn't they let her have her son back?

Thank goodness Mitch had seen the blanket. Two attempts on her life in front of a cop had made Tanner take her more seriously. She couldn't let up, though. If she didn't push, no one would.

Emily shifted her gaze from the search to Mitch, who was focusing intently on his conversation with one of the bomb-squad techs. His ability to ignore the pain he had to be feeling left her in awe. If only he'd lean against the vehicle and ease the weight, but his dogged determination wouldn't let him show any vulnerability. She'd learned that about him in the short time she'd known him.

Her hand slipped into her pocket and pulled out her phone. It had gone dark. The battery must have died. She needed to try Perry again. They were ninety minutes late. Maybe the PI had attempted to call. She got out of the car and walked over to Mitch. "Can I borrow your cell to call Perry?"

His expression more grave than she'd ever seen, Mitch handed her the phone. He clasped her arm and walked her a few feet away from the tech, bending his lips to her ear. The warm breath bathed her neck, and she shivered at his closeness. "Don't tell him where you are. Just set up another meet. We can't be too careful."

Mitch backed away, his expression stonelike and chilled as he continued the conversation with the other officer.

She hated not being able to trust anyone. She stepped a few feet away. Her call went straight to Perry's message. Where was he?

The phone vibrated in her hand and started playing an unrecognizable tune.

"Turn that thing down, bud. You want to make everyone sick with that stupid fight song?"

Emily's gaze flew toward the voice. A striking-looking man walked toward Mitch, grinning and holding a cell in his hand.

"You never did have good taste, Ian."

Ian tapped his phone and Mitch's stopped ringing. His tension eased, and he smiled in a way she'd never seen. He looked at this man with complete trust and confidence. As the strong friendship between the two men became clear, Emily had never felt more alone. Mitch had connections.

She'd witnessed the trust when he'd spoken to a few of the cops. Without hearing a word, the camaraderie between them spoke volumes. How could Mitch ever be totally on her side? He'd saved her life, yes. But he was loyal to them. She should remember that.

"Did you find me a ride?" Mitch said.

Ian grinned with a mischievous glint deep in his eyes.

"Your brother Noah's SUV. He won't miss it."

"True. After that last big software deal, he went nuts and bought the Hummer. He's got five cars now."

Mitch tried to pluck the keys from his friend's hand, but Ian closed his fist. His face turned serious. "It's not every day my best friend's car gets blown to smithereens. What's up, bud?"

Emily's body tensed. How would Mitch respond? Had he believed her?

He looked around at the few cops who still stood near them. "Not now."

The vise around Emily's heart eased a bit. He might. He just might be on her side.

"Then I'm not leaving," Ian said, the keys still in his grip.

Emily recognized the tick in Mitch's jaw. She'd seen it when Ghost had cut the girl, and when he'd studied the pictures of the children on her wall. Friends were too precious. She couldn't be the cause of problems between them.

"It's my fault," Emily said quietly, stepping into their circle. She held out her hand. "Emily Wentworth."

At the mention of her name, Ian paused, the openness in his face evaporating. He reached out his hand to hers. "I've followed your case. Ian Archer. I'm the investigator for the coroner's office."

He'd probably studied the accident. She nodded, trying to gauge his judgment. Was she a black widow to him?

"No matter what you've heard, I didn't kill my husband,"

she said, deciding to meet his doubts head-on. "I just want to find my son. It's starting to look like someone doesn't want me to."

Ian studied her expression, and, as if he had made some decision, his face softened a bit. "I understand. I hope you find him."

She clutched at the small opening. "Did you look into the accident? Was there anything that stood out to you?"

Ian stiffened and slid a sidelong glance to Mitch.

"Emily's private investigator, Perry Young, indicated he had information that there might be some…irregularities in the police work. We were on our way to meet him when—"

"I see. Can I tag along?" Ian asked. "I'd be *very* interested in his theories."

She could use his expertise. "Sure."

"No," Mitch bit out at the same time.

She whirled on him. "Why? If he can help—"

"Ian has a daughter to take care of."

Mitch's face was uncompromising. The friends' gazes held, obviously communicating in a way she didn't understand. Ian finally nodded. "Fine. See you at your dad's for the tree trimming," he said. He turned to Emily. "It's nice to meet you. Good luck."

Ian tossed the set of keys to Mitch before walking away.

"Why did you do that?" she asked. "He might know something or have suspicions about who could be involved."

"He and my goddaughter have been through enough. Too many cops saw him here as it is, and if one of them is our mole, I don't want him associated with a case involving missing children. Understand?"

The fierce protectiveness in his words made her tremble with regret. What had she been thinking? She had no right to bring anyone else into her nightmare. "You're right. I'm sorry. There's no need to put anyone else in danger." She faced Mitch. "Detective Tanner is up that hill. Why not just give the assignment back? I don't really need you. I have Perry. I'll get by."

"I didn't mean it like that. I'll connect with Ian later. I just don't want to be obvious or make Haley a target."

Back stiff, she ignored his words and started toward the crowd of cops. Mitch yanked her arm. "I'm not letting you go," he said, tugging her against him. "You *do* need me. I saw the blanket. I believe you. Do you think these other men will?"

"Perry does. Keep your friends and family close, Mitch. I know what it's like to lose them."

"I'll look out for mine. That doesn't mean I'm going to abandon you. I'm in too deep." He gave her a small smile. "Now let's talk to Perry. He may suspect who wants you dead."

After a quick consultation with Tanner, Mitch led her to his brother's pristine SUV. The recently detailed smell assaulted Emily's memories. Her last fight with Eric had been about the compact. He'd wanted to get her something new. She hadn't wanted to risk it. He'd been furious with her, but she'd known they couldn't afford it. They'd struggled to meet the mortgage when he'd left his father's company. She didn't care, but Eric hadn't been used to budgeting or doing without. She ran her hand over the supple leather seats, and her eyes burned. This vehicle was just her husband's style. Top of the line. All the bells and whistles.

As Mitch steered the car down the mountain, she clutched at the armrests until her fingers hurt. Her breath hitched, and a small sound escaped. She rubbed her eyes. No. She didn't need to think about the past. She had to have faith that with Mitch and Perry she'd put what was left of her family back together.

"You okay?"

Emily cleared her throat. "I'm fine. Perry's office is just around the corner. I don't blame him for not waiting for us, but I wish he'd pick up."

Mitch pulled onto a rundown street. Iron bars decorated most windows. A few unsavory characters loitered on the corners. "He's not exactly in the garden district, is he?"

"He stayed on the case. I'm grateful.

"Just tell me you didn't come here alone."

"Sometimes."

"Emily, you've got to start being more cautious."

"I'll do what I have to do to find my son, Mitch."

One glance at her companion's strong jawline and determined expression reminded her things had changed. Mitch believed in her. She'd given him the out, and he hadn't taken it. He could have. Maybe, just maybe, she'd found an ally who would stick with her. And not because he received a check.

He parallel-parked and stopped the engine before twisting to face her. "I take the lead here."

"He trusts me."

"Precisely why I do the talking this time. I'll put some pressure on him, but I want to know if he's blowing smoke or not." Mitch's eyes grew cold, and his expression dangerous. "If we're really dealing with a breach in the department, I want to know now."

As charming as Mitch could be—and Emily had to admit, she liked him—he had that deadly look that she'd hate to be on the wrong side of.

They climbed up the stairs, and Emily kept a close eye on his gait. She could see a bit of strain, but he powered through the stiffness, not giving away anything. One more thing to appreciate about him—he had grit.

Mitch turned a corner. Perry's office door was cracked open. And quiet. Mitch paused. His entire body tensed; his stance screamed alert. He leaned forward. "You ever seen the door ajar?" His voice was so quiet she could barely hear him.

He pointed to the other doors down the hall. All of them were closed. She strained to remember.

"No," she whispered. "I've always knocked."

"Stay behind me."

He moved in front of her and pulled a gun from beneath his jacket. With caution, he eased toward the office. His back against the wall, he slowly pushed at the wood.

He stepped through the entrance and stilled.

Emily peeked around him.

Perry Young faced them, on his knees, his face bruised, his nose bleeding, his hands behind his head.

A masked figure stood behind the PI, a gun at his head.

Perry lifted resigned eyes and met Emily's gaze.

"Eighty-five!" he yelled.

The gun went off.

Chapter Five

Perry Young's face exploded. Blown off too fast for Mitch to pull the trigger at the killer. He shoved Emily into the hall and aimed his Glock. "Denver police. Put the gun down. Now."

The man leaped over Perry's rickety desk and crashed through the window. Mitch skidded across the old wood floor, hitching through the opening onto the fire escape. The perp bounded down to the first landing and then hurtled to the ground.

Mitch eyed the distance. Too far. He took the steps as quickly as possible, cursing every one. A few months ago, he would've had this guy the second the assassin hit the brown, winter grass. Mitch jumped the last few stairs and landed on the turf. His leg seized, but he ignored the pain. Some kids stood staring, a soccer ball rolling across the yard. Mitch couldn't risk a shot. He gripped his gun as the man raced past the group.

Mitch's legs pumped hard in pursuit as the kids scattered, but the man shot off like he was used to doing hundred-yard sprints. Within seconds the killer shoved through a fence. By the time Mitch slammed open the gate, his quarry had disappeared. A motorcycle revved and peeled away, but Mitch couldn't see anything through the thicket of trees guarding the street.

Cursing, Mitch slipped his gun back into the holster. What good was rehab if he couldn't run down a murder suspect?

And he'd left Emily alone.

Mitch raced back to Perry's office, using the stairs this time to preserve the scene. Expecting to see her trembling in the hallway, his gut fell when he reached the second floor. Empty. Silent.

Had the whole thing been a diversion? Had someone else been waiting to take her?

He redrew his weapon and entered the room. There she was, behind Perry's desk, rifling through the papers. Not just papers. Evidence.

"What are you doing? This is a crime scene."

"He's my last connection." Emily tore through another drawer, eyes wild with desperation, her movements frantic. "There has to be something here. Something about Joshua. The tattoo. The cops."

Mitch limped around the desk. He tugged at her hands, enclosing them in his fists, and pulled her away from the stack of papers. "Look at me, Emily." She raised her gaze to his, and he released one hand to let his finger run down her cheek. "Let's go into the hall and call for the crime-scene unit."

She tugged away from him. "Don't treat me like I'm a fragile doll. I'm not."

Her hand hovered over her throat as her husky voice cracked a bit—a stark reminder of just how much she'd endured.

"Perry can't just be gone." She stared at his body.

The killer had used a hollow point. The PI hadn't stood a chance. Her face lost all color, but she didn't look away.

"He told me to come alone. To tell no one." She rounded on Mitch. "You heard him. Did you reveal to *anyone* where we were going? Tanner, maybe?"

The unspoken accusation hung like poison between them, her suspicions palpable. Mitch stiffened, but as he stared at what was left of Perry's head, and the blood and brain splattered across the floor, his mind clicked through the possibilities of who might have known of their destination. Ian knew. Tanner knew. If his boss had told anyone…She had every right to be distrustful.

So did Mitch.

Until he was sure who had killed Perry and tried to kill Emily, he had to be extremely cautious. He couldn't trust the police department. The realization skewered his gut.

Mitch guided her into the hallway, pressed close against him. "A few months ago, I would've ignored the suggestion someone I know could be responsible for attacking you. Or for killing Perry. Since then, the man I trusted more than anyone on the force set me up for an ambush. He caused this." Mitch tapped his bad leg. "I'm not discounting anything anymore." He turned Emily in his arms. "That means we're on our own. Fewer resources to find your son until we're certain who our friends are. Can you live with that?"

"Perry paid with his life for helping me. It's my fault. I can't ask you to take that same risk."

Her voice had turned monotone. Shock had settled in.

"His death's not your fault. Blame the guy who pulled the trigger." He willed her to look at him until the cloudy, stunned look faded from her expression. "I will tell you one thing, though. This means Perry was onto something. He discovered a connection he shouldn't have, and they wanted him silenced."

Mitch pulled out his cell phone, and Emily stilled his hand.

"Who are you calling?"

"The police. I have to notify them of the shooting. No choice. If I don't, someone else will, and we can be placed here."

Mitch didn't like the churning in his gut. He studied Emily's jittery movements as he made the call. Her life was at stake. He couldn't let her down, so he'd have to accept the weight of his deception. Until he could uncover the truth.

"They'll be here in a few minutes. I need you to think back to every conversation you've had with Perry in the past month."

Emily bit down on the side of her lip, concentrating. "He got real excited about Sister Kate's shelter. Said things didn't smell right there. You heard the phone call. Oh, he really wanted me to get a good look at Ghost's tattoo."

Pain flashed in her eyes, and she massaged her temple. Mitch had seen that look before. When he'd pushed her to remember that night, she'd had the same expression.

"You're starting to remember," he said.

"A red and green tattoo. Some kind of figure, I think."

"What else did Perry tell you?" Mitch asked.

"I don't know. I took notes. They're at the house."

"How about the number he yelled right before—"

Emily's eyes cleared. "Eighty-five! His code. He talked about how when he got tidbits of information, he never wanted to be the only one who had them. He stashed them away."

"Good for Perry. Do you know where he kept the files?"

"He told me if anything ever happened to him, to remember that a sommelier would find the files before the bad guys."

"He hid his evidence in his wine rack?"

"I don't know." Panic laced her voice. "Oh, God. He never told me his hiding place."

"What about your contract? Paperwork he gave you?"

Her vision cleared. "Maybe. He wouldn't have just said that word without thinking I could find it, right?"

"Exactly. Let's search for a liquor stash in his office. The guy was an alcoholic from what I gather. We'll find it." He glanced at his watch and held her shoulders. Mitch whistled through his teeth. "Listen to me carefully. I can't touch the evidence in that room. Rules, you know." He slipped on a pair of gloves that hadn't been standard issue for him until he'd been benched from SWAT. "But your fingerprints are already on his desk. So…"

He watched her eyes widen with comprehension. She hurried back inside Perry's office, avoiding the body on the floor, but focused. His Emily was fearless.

He followed her into the room. They rifled through papers and opened drawers, but there was nothing helpful. No wine bottles, just a half-full flask of whisky. No address of a store. He shook his head at Perry's body. The man had a code word. That meant he had a plan. He had to have left a clue somewhere.

Sirens screamed in the distance.

"We're out of time." Mitch tugged Emily's hand and started toward the exit.

She tugged one last time on a last locked drawer before grabbing a letter opener and jimmying the lock. She snagged a small box containing files, notes and an unopened bottle of wine. She gave him a challenging look. He sighed, then nodded.

"What about his apartment?" she said. "Can we go there, too?"

"The investigators'll be all over his place. We'll stash the box in my SUV and wait for the cops downstairs. Then we go to your place and look at the evidence and your notes. Maybe we'll get lucky. I'll keep an eye on the investigation. If they find liquor bottles, I'll know about it."

"But you won't tell Tanner, right?"

Her voice made his skin prickle. He didn't like not trusting his colleagues. The men he'd put his life on the line for a hundred times.

"For now."

"I CAN'T GET PERRY out of my mind," Emily said quietly as Mitch maneuvered the SUV up the road toward her house. The image of his faceless body chilled her far more than the winter that had taken hold, or the clearing of leafless aspens poking through the surrounding pines.

They'd spent too long giving statements to the police. After a scathing lecture, Tanner had warned both of them not to leave town, informing them they were persons of interest in Perry's execution.

She pictured his endearing face, his ruddy cheeks, the deep crow's-feet at the corner of his eyes, the eagerness with which he came to her to give her one more bit of news. The excitement in his final phone call.

"His last words were to help me."

"And we won't let him down," Mitch said. "We'll find out what got him killed."

"And make them pay." She twisted in her seat. "I want them to pay for taking the life of an innocent man. He didn't have to die."

Mitch squeezed her hand. "We'll figure this out, Emily. I won't stop until we do."

She stared at his large, strong fingers engulfing hers. She believed him. He wouldn't give up. Not like William or even Eric had. The Wentworth brothers had both gone down the path of least resistance—Eric by avoiding his family, William by giving into them. Mitch would never have done either. He didn't walk away from a fight, he ran toward conflict and battled it out. He was a protector, a warrior. Perhaps that's why she felt safe when she was near him.

She gripped him hard as a familiar stretch of road loomed around the next corner. The police had removed the signs of the roadside investigation. Only the scarred pavement where the cars had burned remained. A few hundred feet farther, a white cross rose in the gravel.

A barren cross.

"They took the poinsettias," Emily whispered.

"Evidence. I'm sorry."

"I need to replace them," she said quietly as they passed the memorial. "Eric's favorite."

"I'll take you to a florist's," Mitch said as he turned onto her street. "Whose car is outside your house?" His voice had tensed; his hands gripped the steering wheel as if he were ready to spin the SUV around.

Emily turned. A familiar black Mercedes sat running at the front curb. She didn't need to see inside its tinted windows to know who waited for her. "Oh, no. Not today."

"Who is it?"

"Victoria. The woman who believes I'm the worst thing that ever happened to her family—especially Eric." Emily swiped at the errant hairs and the char and dirt on her clothes. Nothing like looking as if she'd just climbed out of a ditch to give her oh-so-perfect mother-in-law more ammunition.

Emily bit her lip and slid a glance to Mitch. "Do you mind staying in the car while I get rid of her?"

"Yes, actually I do. I'm interested in what Mrs. Wentworth has to say. Like how far she'd go to make you look suspicious. And why she happens by for a visit on the day you were almost killed."

The implication of his words sent waves of shock through Emily. No way. The Wentworths wouldn't risk anything that could cost them an ounce of respect.

Mitch pulled the SUV into the driveway. Just as he and Emily exited the vehicle, a driver opened the back door of the Mercedes. Victoria Wentworth stepped out and paused. Her simple black Chanel suit said much more in subtlety than her biting insults said with a smile. She waited, clearly expecting the peons to approach her. Emily sighed and started to her, but Mitch grabbed her hand and tugged her back.

"I don't want you out in the open. Go inside. She can come to you."

"You don't understand—"

Mitch's eyes twinkled a bit, and Emily recognized that hint of mischief behind the layers of steel. "Oh, I comprehend the situation quite well. Get in the house, Emily."

She turned to the front door before she realized she didn't have her keys. Quickly, she fished the spare from beneath a pot on the front porch. She chanced a glance back at Mitch, and he shook his head, clearly frustrated that she had stashed the item in such an obvious place. Well, at least she didn't have to break into the house.

She opened the door and slipped inside. Home. Finally. She so desperately needed to be here. Safe. Secure.

With more than a little curiosity at how Mitch would handle the formidable Mrs. Wentworth, Emily peered out the window at the driveway. Mitch's conversation with her mother-in-law would've been worth a front-row seat, especially since Victoria had actually let him escort her up the sidewalk.

How long had it been since the Wentworths had set foot in this house? Maybe only once in her and Eric's three-year marriage?

"I appreciate your understanding, Mrs. Wentworth. In re-opening the investigation into Eric's death, we want nothing more than to find out what happened."

Mitch's smooth voice filtered through the open doorway. As he escorted Victoria into Emily's house, she bristled. What was he up to? Victoria had made it perfectly clear what she wanted: Emily to pay for Eric's death.

"Well, I'm not one to speak out of school, but I'm quite dismayed to see you accompanying Emily. She should be your prime suspect. Look at what she did today. Trying to sell Eric's home. It's disgraceful, and I'm going to put a stop to it."

"Now, ma'am. You know that I have to keep my options open." She'd never seen Mitch smile like that. It didn't reach his eyes. Each movement, each gesture was calculated and focused. Mitch led Victoria into the house's formal living room to the sofa that faced a photograph of Emily and Eric. He pulled up a chair as her mother-in-law settled into her seat but made sure she could see the happy picture. Emily recognized the ploy. He *wanted* a reaction from Eric's mother.

"I'd like to hear your thoughts," he said. "About your son."

Mitch's voice held just the right note of sympathy. He turned his face away from Victoria to Emily and gave her a small wink. "Could you fix your mother-in-law some hot tea, please? It's cold outside."

Amazing. He manipulated like a pro. Emily didn't know what he expected to gain, but she'd let him have his way. For now. "Certainly."

She pulled out a small, antique teapot she and Eric had found in a little shop on their honeymoon and set the water to boiling before edging back into the room where Mitch played Victoria like a Stradivarius. He charmed the woman. Emily placed her fingers to the lips he'd almost kissed. He'd done the same with her.

"I told Eric not to marry a girl like that, but he wouldn't listen. He was young, idealistic."

"Sounds like he was a good son."

"Perfect. The best son any mother could ever want. Until he met *her*. He stopped coming by to visit. We never saw him anymore."

Mitch laid his hand on Victoria's. "You miss him."

For the first time in a year, Emily really studied Victoria's features. Grief had etched lines in her formerly smooth face. Why couldn't they have clung to each other? That's all

Emily had ever wanted. Acceptance. Support. To be part of a family again.

"She was so intent on getting the insurance money." Victoria's face turned harsh. "That's when I was certain what I'd always suspected was true. She never loved Eric. She loved the Wentworth money. And now she's selling *his* house. She's throwing away his memory."

"That's not true."

Emily stalked into the room. She couldn't take the attacks anymore. "I *never* cared about the money for myself. I just want to find Joshua."

"Then why was *William* paying for plane tickets and bills for that private investigator?"

"To search for *your* grandson." Emily looked down at Victoria. "I want him back."

For a moment, she thought Victoria's expression softened a bit. Then that haughty look reappeared. "No. I'm not wrong. I know your kind. You care about nothing if you'll sell everything Eric ever gave to you." She faced Mitch. "You look into the $250,000 account I found. It's in *her* name. Not Eric's." Then she turned to Emily, her gaze as icy as her heart. "When you can explain that away, I *might* believe you weren't responsible for killing my son."

She rose and walked out the door, regal as ever.

Mitch whistled under his breath. "Wow. She doesn't mince words."

"I told you." The kettle shrieked from the kitchen. Emily hurried to remove the pot from the stove. He followed her. The room suddenly seemed much smaller, claustrophobic even. Maybe it was the low ceilings, but his muscular frame and larger-than-life presence sucked the air from her lungs.

"Want some?" she asked, her voice strangely breathless.

"The tea is for you. I figured you'd need it after your mother-in-law left, and I was pretty sure she'd leave before it was ready. I just wanted you out of the room. So, about the $250,000—"

Emily faced Mitch. "If I'd had access to that kind of money, do you think I'd be selling my house to pay for the investigation? The house Eric and I built together? I didn't even know about the money until today." She struggled to swallow back the sob that stuck in her throat. No. She couldn't let herself regret what had to happen. Without William's support, or Perry, she could at least count on the money from the house to help her find Joshua.

Mitch lifted his hand to her cheek. "I'm on your side," he said softly. "Remember that."

She nodded.

"Did anyone ask for your signature on anything unusual?"

The question harkened back to Dane Tanner's interrogation. Her entire body tensed, her neck muscles bunched in resistance.

"Remember," Mitch whispered.

His hands moved to her shoulders, kneaded the knots. She sighed at the comforting touch. She didn't know what good her answer would be.

"I've signed a million forms since Eric died. I signed papers to try to refinance the physical-therapy business. I don't remember opening a bank account." She lifted her gaze to his. "I saw the signature. It can't be mine. It looks like mine, but I didn't sign it."

"The account existed before the accident. This isn't something recent, Emily. I'll get the exact date from Tanner. Maybe that will jog your memory."

She couldn't stand so close to him any longer. She turned away and hugged her arms around herself. "Why is this happening?"

Mitch moved in closer, but she stiffened, trying to ignore the longing that had bubbled up inside of her, that still threatened to escape. She pulled a teabag out of the cupboard and poured hot water in a flowered cup.

Emily inhaled the floral scent of the herb drink, but it didn't comfort, soothe or distract her. She felt his warm presence again at her back. Her body tingled. He wouldn't give up. His persistence was one of his most irritating—and appealing—qualities. His heat warmed her from shoulders to hips. She wanted nothing more than to give in to her instincts, to sag against him, let him wrap her in a cocoon and make the world go away for just a few minutes, a few hours.

Gently, almost tentatively, he rested his hands on her shoulders again. "We'll get through this," he whispered, his warm breath at her ear.

His hands eased down her arms. She could've escaped at any moment. He would've let her go, but she wanted his touch. She needed his strength. She'd been alone for so long, battling the world for too long. For this moment, in this small room, she truly believed she'd found a champion. She and Mitch against a world gone crazy.

Effortlessly, he folded her against him, his hard body cradling the softness of her own. Her hands shook. His warm hands surrounded hers, and he took the cup in his hands and set it aside before turning her in his arms.

His chocolate-brown eyes had gone black with desire. His body fairly pulsed with need. He lifted her chin, and his finger toyed with a strand of hair near her face.

She understood passion. The electric longing had crackled between them before. But this was different. He could have swept her into his arms, tugged her to him and taken her lips. She would've given him what they both wanted, but he didn't. His hands worked slowly up and down her arms, then around her back to her shoulders, touching her with such a gentle persuasion that she melted deep in her belly.

Her heart pounded and she leaned into him, wanting his

heat to warm her from the inside out, needing to feel safe. He was the only one who could give her that. "Please," she said.

A small smile tilted his lips. "Please what?"

"Hold me."

With a groan, he secured her hard against him. She could feel every plane of his body, the muscles in his arms and chest. She hugged him close. He shivered, and a surge of female pride raced through her. She'd made *him* tremble.

What if she raised her head? Would he kiss her? Would he want her?

His hips arched against her. Yes, he wanted her, and he wasn't afraid of letting her know it. The loneliness of the past year crashed over her. Dare she risk letting herself care, or even feel something more than grief and emptiness?

The chimes of the grandfather clock shattered the moment.

He rested his forehead against hers. "It's too fast, isn't it, Emily?"

She bit her lip and nodded. He glanced at his phone. "I need to make a call. Drink your tea. And someday soon… maybe it won't be too fast."

He caressed her cheek and left the room, the phone at his ear. "This had better be good."

Emily sucked in a deep breath. Her nerve endings tingled. She paced the floor and noticed the message indicator on the phone she'd put in the charger. She couldn't believe she hadn't noticed. She dialed her voice mail.

"Mrs. Wentworth."

Perry's voice sounded through the speakerphone.

She staggered at the sound of the dead man's words.

"You didn't show up, and your cell went straight to voice mail. Call me as soon as you get the message. This thing is bigger than I thought, ma'am. Lots of money. Lots of influence. I confirmed the Denver PD is involved, but I don't know the cop's name yet."

A harsh curse sounded from across the room. Mitch had come back. A frown creased his face, and the muscle in his jaw throbbed.

Perry's voice continued. "Ghost shouldn't have escaped. Someone set it up." A bit of rustling shifted through the phone. "If something happens to me…you'll know what I know. I don't want to say more on the phone." Perry paused. "Be careful, Mrs. Wentworth. Don't trust anyone. Call me."

Emily sagged against the counter.

Mitch strode across the room to her. "Timing hasn't been on our side, has it?" He kissed her cheek, letting his lips linger there. "Remember where we were."

He lifted the cup and pushed it into her hands. "Now, take a sip and let's go through your notes so we can find Perry's evidence."

Emily clasped the tea and walked down the short hallway toward the dining room, Mitch at her heels. She slid open the door and the teacup fell from her fingertips, shattering on the hardwood floor. "No!"

The walls were barren. The boxes gone. Every piece of evidence, every notebook, every pushpin, everything she'd gathered over the past nine months, vanished.

Stolen.

Mitch dragged her toward the door. "We're getting out of here. Now!"

Chapter Six

Emily dug her heels into the floor and yanked out of Mitch's hold. "Wait a minute. We can't just leave—"

"Someone tried to blow your car up today," he snapped. "We're leaving until the bomb squad clears this place."

Her eyes widened. "Wait." She scooped up the teddy bear and two picture frames and threw them in a bag. "I'm not going without these," she said, her eyes fierce.

Mitch clutched Emily's hand and yanked her across the kitchen. No way was he retracing steps through the house. They'd have to make do without their coats.

She snagged her cell phone and charger. "But what about—"

"No time, Emily. We're not taking any more chances."

He dragged her to the back exit. After a quick inspection of the hinges and frame for a trip wire, he flung open the oak door. He couldn't believe he'd been so careless. They'd meandered around the house for a half hour. Making tea, for God's sake. A device set to the gas stove and it would have been all over. They'd both be dead, and no one would know someone had cleaned out all the evidence from her dining room.

She stumbled outside after him, their feet crunching on the leftover snow. He scanned the perimeter of the yard, searching for footprints or anything out of place.

No disturbances. The perp had probably come in through the front.

"I'm sorry," Mitch said. "I should've scoped out the house before you entered. I let you down. It won't happen again."

"The house was locked," she protested. "How did they—"

"When's the last time you used the key under the pot?"

She flushed.

"That's what I figured. You're a smart woman, Emily. You handled yourself well downtown, but you can't lower your guard, even on your home turf. Not ever. Now, we have to get out of here."

He picked his way around the side of the house. His body tensed with awareness, he tugged her near. "Stay close to me."

Emily's hand rested lightly against his back. He needed to feel her presence, to know she was safe. He'd rely on his SWAT instincts. Those he could trust. Clearly his detective intuition didn't make the grade. When he reached the corner, Mitch stilled, listening for any sign, searching for any movement.

She trembled against him. He gave her a comforting squeeze. "Let me check the SUV, and then we're out of here."

She nodded, and he did a quick sweep underneath the vehicle. Looked clean, but he gave it a second pass anyway. He couldn't be too careful. He motioned her toward the vehicle and opened the door. She jumped in, and he slid behind the steering wheel.

Clutching the bag with the photos to her as if they were a lifeline to her memories, she fastened her safety belt.

Within a minute, they were on the road, Mitch on high alert and determined that no one would catch him unaware again.

Emily peeked around. "What are we going to do?"

"First off, I'm hiding you someplace safe. Then we'll

figure out exactly what you've stumbled onto. Because it's big. And worth killing over."

Emily clutched the bear to her chest. "I should never have asked for your help. I didn't know it would get this dangerous for you. If you want out, I understand."

Mitch didn't like how her words cut him straight through to his heart. He shouldn't feel so much—except he couldn't believe that she'd said something so incredibly dense. His anger was about more than just her putting herself in danger. She had him. He was with her all the way. Until she was safe. Until she found out what happened to her son. But she didn't believe in him.

"I am not going anywhere. Get used to it."

"But—"

"Subject closed."

Mitch checked the rear- and side-view mirrors every couple of seconds. The neighborhood streets were abandoned. To his surprise, his Neanderthal declaration seemed to ease the tension in the car rather than ratchet it up. Maybe Emily wasn't as ready to go it alone as she wanted to appear.

"I wonder if I'll ever see my home again," she said, finally breaking the silence.

"I don't know." He wouldn't stop being honest. At least about some things. "If all the bad guys wanted was your research, they got that."

"The whole thing is so bizarre. Nothing was disturbed in the rest of the house. If we hadn't gone into the dining room, we wouldn't even have known."

"Since they took your research, you either found something or came close to exposing someone. Whoever did this thought you died in the explosion, or else emptied the house right after we left. If he'd succeeded in killing you, the cops wouldn't have known there was a home invasion or that anything was missing."

Emily sighed. "Very few people know about the room. If I died, there'd be no one to look for Joshua anymore."

She shivered, her eyes huge in her pale face.

Mitch's heart twisted as he thought of just how close she'd come to getting killed on his watch. Again. "I'll always look, Emily. No matter what."

She drew out the photo of an infant, gently touching the face. "Perry told me he would find Joshua. He had a lead, and he sounded very confident this time." She glanced at Mitch. "What was *your* phone call about?"

"Nothing helpful. Tanner letting me know that Ghost is still at large. There have been alleged sightings downtown and one near Sister Kate's, but nothing concrete."

"What if we can't find Ghost? All the evidence was back at my house."

"Not everything. We didn't take Perry's box inside." Mitch cocked his head. "Our luck could be changing."

Emily sank into the soft leather seats. "Where are we going? Your place?"

"Not secure enough, especially if there's a cop informant like Perry said. We'll head to my brother Noah's house. He *loaned* us the car. Might as well put us up, too. What he doesn't know when he's traveling to every corner of the world won't hurt him."

"What if they find us?" she said softly. "I don't want to cause trouble for you or your family."

Mitch exited toward Boulder. "Noah's place is like Fort Knox. Gated community, high-tech alarm system, video surveillance around the perimeter. No one can get in. Not without us being aware."

"Maybe I should find my own—"

"Do you have somewhere you can go that would be safe?" He said the words gently.

"Sister Kate," she said, her voice hesitating.

"Not with Ghost on the loose. Besides, the threats on your life started after you began working with Sister Kate's girls, right?"

Emily nodded.

"Enough said." Mitch pulled up at a booth to a gated community, and the guard waved him past.

"He let *you* in without showing an ID," she said.

"I watch Noah's place when he's gone. And play with some of his toys. He's got a killer man cave. Don't worry. No one else gets in."

Mitch pulled onto a long drive past a series of oaks and flicked open the SUV's console. He pressed a remote control and one of five garage doors rose. "I don't want any sign someone's home," he said as the door closed behind them.

He escorted her into the house, past a large interior courtyard with an Olympic-size pool. At her dropped jaw, he laughed. "Yeah, Noah went a little overboard on the decoration. You should see the hot tub. Looks like it's in the middle of Belize."

He placed the box they'd taken from Perry's house on a huge dining table, then started toward the kitchen. "You hungry?"

They could both use some food. And a distraction.

He turned, and Emily held the two photos and the teddy bear with its unique one blue eye and one brown eye tightly in her arms. She looked lost.

"You don't think we'll find Joshua, do you? Not really." She took in a shuddering breath. "I need the truth."

The vulnerability in her words shook him. He wanted to tell her yes, more than anything. Instead, he settled for the truth. "We have a chance." He walked to her, then gently tucked some errant strands of hair behind her ear. "And we will explore every lead we find, no matter who wants us to stop. That, I promise you, Emily, is the truth." He cupped her cheek and looked directly into her eyes, unblinking. "We can relax, have a good meal, do whatever we want. No one will bother us here."

She nodded as he tugged her toward an overstuffed sofa that looked like it might swallow her up. She settled on the edge, awkward and tense. He rested his hand on her back and circled in slow, deliberate movements. Her back stiffened, muscles tightening, but she didn't pull away.

"We're safe here? Really?" she asked.

Mitch nodded. "Yes."

"I could use a shower...." Her voice trailed off. "Except I don't have clothes or a nightgown or a toothbrush. Or anything." She looked at Mitch. "I feel like I'm drifting...rudderless," she said finally.

Mitch couldn't bear it. He reached for her hand and held it tight. "Look at what's happened in the past two days. Most people would've broken, but you've been astonishing. Strong. Tough."

She pulled away from him. "I don't feel tough. I feel as if I could shatter into a million pieces. That's not like me. I need to pull it together."

Mitch leaned toward her and twisted the soft strands of her hair, taking in the dark circles beneath her cobalt eyes, the strain around her mouth, the tension in her neck. "You need food and sleep."

He brushed his thumb against the soft skin of her temple, and she closed her eyes.

"Not yet," she whispered. "Can you just...be with me... quietly for a minute? 'Til I relax."

He shifted and lay down on the huge soft cushions with her tucked against him. "Like this?"

With a sigh, she sagged against him, her softness pressed close. "Yes."

They lay there silently for several minutes. He relished just holding her. Any other time, he would've been desperate to kiss her, to have her beneath him, passionately holding him, but he simply studied her features and enjoyed the feel of her against him.

How long had it been since he'd cuddled next to a woman and said absolutely nothing? How comfortable. How strange.

And yet, intense desire throbbed just beneath the craving he now had for her. One touch, one kiss, one seductive glance and his instincts would take over.

He shifted his hips away from her so she wouldn't feel the power of his desire. She didn't need anything but to feel safe.

She opened her eyes and stared at him.

"I've thought a few times that you might kiss me," she said softly.

"Have you wanted me to?"

"Sometimes," she said. "But my emotions are all over the place. I've been alone so long, I'm not sure I remember how to handle any of this. Or to know if you're even interested in me."

He shifted his body, and her eyes widened as he let her feel his need. "Don't ever doubt that I want you, Emily."

Nervous, she raised her hand to his cheek. "You need a shave. That will tickle."

"Let's check." Mitch nuzzled her neck, and she giggled. Within moments, her laughter gave way to sighs as he let his lips softly explore her jaw, her cheek, until his lips finally found hers. His body sang as she opened to him and he delved inside, exploring her sweet honey. It was as if he'd been waiting to taste her for his entire life.

She eased beneath him, and his hips settled into the cradle of her.

He raised his head and stared into her eyes. She wanted him, but something made him pull away.

He touched her hair and closed his eyes and the silky

strands slid through his fingertips. With a gentle kiss he rose from the couch and held out his hand.

"The shower's down the hall, second door on the right. Go."

"Did I do something wrong?"

"No, Emily, and I don't want to, either, so take a hot shower. I'll take a cold one."

Her gaze dropped down his body, and he knew he couldn't hide his reaction to her. Her cheeks blossomed, and she quickly headed for Noah's hallway.

"Mitch?" she said, turning back to him. "I still don't have anything to wear."

"I'll find some of my sister Sierra's clothes and leave them beside the door. Towels are in the bathroom." He nodded toward the guest room. "Go on. Afterward, help yourself to whatever is in the fridge. I'll probably soak in the hot tub for a while."

"Okay. Thanks." Emily's gaze slid southward again, triggering another response from Mitch, and she all but ran down the hall.

Cursing his suddenly chivalrous streak, Mitch turned away. He could've seduced her. Why hadn't he? She could be beneath him right now, writhing under his caress. He knew how to please a woman, make her want him, make her glad she'd spent the night with him as her lover. And he'd pushed her away. Why?

Because she's not ready.

And she's not a woman to make love to for fun. She was a forever kind of woman.

Off-limits. Unless he wanted more.

He clutched at his leg and massaged the sore thigh muscle. He couldn't want more. Not until he was whole again.

Not until he discovered who was after her. Not until he found her son.

Not until he could tell her the truth.

From the guest room, a shower turned on. Emily was in there, undressed, wet, waiting. And off-limits.

EMILY LET THE STEAMING water sluice over her, relaxing her neck, her back, her arms. Finally, she'd eliminated the smell of burning plastic from her nostrils. As she soaped her body, she remembered Mitch's hands on her, his gentle touch, his tenderness.

He was a good man. She'd seen the flare of desire in his eyes, but he'd let her take the lead. Part of her wished he hadn't. What if he'd simply stripped away her clothes and seduced her with all of the skill she knew he possessed.

She would have melted in his arms. She knew it.

And maybe regretted it. Something he'd been fully aware of. So, he'd hidden his passion with sensitivity, and doing so made her heart race for him all the more.

She stepped out of the shower and wrapped her body in a towel. When she entered the guest room, several sets of jeans, turtlenecks and sweaters had miraculously appeared on the satin-covered bed, along with a nightshirt. The idea that Mitch had been that close to her while she'd been naked in the shower did funny things to her stomach. What would she have done if he'd opened the bathroom door and come in? Would she have been brave enough to open the curtain? Ask him to join her?

Oh, my, what was she thinking?

She laid the extra clothes on a chair and slipped into the nightshirt. The feeling of the cloth on her sensitized skin let her know she'd better get herself under control before she did something stupid. She should be exhausted, but her mind whirled with crazy thoughts. She couldn't imagine even trying to sleep. She didn't want to be alone. And yet, she knew what would happen if she searched out Mitch. The very thing she wanted, and probably shouldn't have.

Taking a deep breath, she crossed to the door and slowly pulled it open. Silence and shadows greeted her. She could barely make out Perry's box on the dining-room table. She picked it up and carried it into the guest room.

Moving the satin comforter to the side, Emily tugged off the lid. She pulled out the wine bottle she'd seen earlier. Sealed. She grabbed a half-full flask and sighed with the knowledge that Perry's demons had clearly been with him constantly. She scanned several pages of barely decipherable handwritten notes that had to do with following some guy to Florida.

Several minutes later she picked up a receipt from a wine shop, and the memory of a story Perry had told her recently clicked. Yes! This could be the clue they needed to move on.

Unable to contain her excitement, she ran out of her room. Where was Mitch? She knocked softly on a bedroom door just down from her own. No answer. Then she heard music drifting from beyond the swimming pool.

She followed the sound until she reached the infamous hot tub. And Mitch. His dark head rested against the tile edge. The bubbling water was nestled among tropical plants, palms, orchids and other brightly colored flowers she'd never seen before. Mitch's brother had created a jungle paradise inside his house, but when she studied Mitch's face, expecting to see pure pleasure, she found tight lines of pain around his mouth, a furrow in his brow.

She'd known he was stoic, but he obviously had no intention of letting anyone know the true extent of his pain. After all the activity, his leg had to be hurting badly, because he looked like he was in agony. Well, he wasn't the only stubborn person around here.

She walked across the tile and slipped into the water, her nightgown clinging to her frame.

"The water feels good," she said quietly. "Is it helping your muscles?"

Mitch snapped upright, his hands dragging a towel into the water and covering his lap. "I thought you'd gone to bed."

"I couldn't sleep, so I looked through Perry's box. I found a receipt, Mitch. For a wine-storage facility." She couldn't stop the grin.

Mitch shifted in the water, maneuvering himself so he sat directly opposite her. "Another lead. That's good."

She slid around the edge of the water. "Your leg's giving you trouble?"

"Not really. Just trying to relax."

"I could help."

"Emily," Mitch warned, "I used up most of my self-restraint when I let you go the last time."

She moved closer and closer, until she was within arm's length. This time, he didn't back away. Cautiously, she placed her hands on his right thigh. The muscles rippled beneath her touch. "You've saved my life, you're helping me find my son."

"It's my job."

"Ouch. Okay, if that's the way we're going to play it, I'm your therapist. This is my job. Now shut up and let me do this."

She moved closer, and with small circular movements, Emily worked the muscles, nightgown floating around her. His skin was taut beneath her fingers, his thigh firm and strong, even as she felt the damaged fibers knot and tug in resistance to her ministrations. Gradually, the tensions began to ease a bit. Emily was very aware of every breath Mitch took. Of the way his strong dark hands gripped the edge of the hot tub as if he fought not to reach for her.

Her movements grew slower, then stopped. She took in a

deep breath, and Mitch moved, lightning fast, his own breathing shallow and more rapid than before.

Silently, Mitch grabbed the material of her nightgown and slid it back through the water until his hands rested on the wall on either side of her waist, the wet cloth of her gown pressed against her. She looked down and realized the thin material left no covering at all. She was practically nude.

Her heart pounded, and she lifted her gaze to his. His chocolate eyes had gone hooded and black. She could feel the desire pulsing through him. As her hands moved over his thigh, she brushed against the towel in his lap, and unintentionally the hardness beneath it. He sucked in a sharp breath.

"My leg is better, Emily. And if you don't plan on taking this all the way, you need to leave. Now. I'm not a slave to my anatomy, but even I have my limits, and you just reached them."

Emily bit her lip. He was giving her a choice. Was she ready? She so wanted to be. She wanted to feel alive again. Could she take a chance? She searched his passion-filled face, full of question, anticipation and desire. "I want—"

Mitch's phone vibrated on the alcove just left of his shoulder. He groaned. "You have got to be kidding," Mitch said crossly. He glanced at the screen, then back at her with regret. "This is work. Another case. I have to take it."

He turned his back and pulled himself out of the water. His back and arm muscles rippled. She averted her gaze, but not before she saw one very toned backside.

He quickly wrapped a towel around his waist, though it couldn't hide his body's response to her. "I'm sorry," he said softly. "You'll never know how much. I'll talk to you in the morning."

Mitch walked away from the hot tub and the temptation that was Emily. He watched as she got up and left, never once looking back. He'd very nearly succumbed to her seduction.

She'd wanted him. And yet, he'd resisted. Had he gone completely crazy?

Mitch tapped the mute off button. "If you're not calling with something important, you're a dead man, Ian."

His best friend was silent for a moment. "Guess there's no point in asking if I can come over and get in some game time while Noah's away." He cleared his throat. "I have the girl's identity. I thought you'd want to know."

Mitch's jaw clenched, and he prayed silently. "Who?"

"Vanessa Colby. She ran away from home about seven months ago."

Mitch let relief wash over him, followed immediately by guilt. "When she found out she was pregnant?"

"Bingo. She wasn't a street girl. At least not until recently."

Mitch breathed out a harsh curse. "That fits with what I learned at the shelter. Any idea what killed her?"

"No obvious injuries, though I found one injection site with some bruising. Could indicate a minor struggle. Toxicology's our last chance to determine cause of death."

Mitch would bet nothing would come of the testing, either. These people were smart. They tried to make murder look like accidents. But he still couldn't quite pinpoint the connection to Emily. She broke the pattern. "Still no sign of Vanessa's baby?"

"Not in the morgue. Unless something's turned up in your department."

Mitch paced the poolroom, his body still throbbing with unfilled desire.

"Hey, you okay?"

"Fine," he said, irritated. "Who do you trust in the police department?"

"Besides you?"

Ian didn't even seem surprised Mitch was alluding to corruption in the Denver PD. Not a good sign. His friend didn't speak for a moment. Mitch waited.

Finally, Ian sighed. "Honestly? If you're wondering about corruption, I'd call your dad."

"He's been out since the accident. Three years is too long."

"When's the last time you talked to him? He's not as out of the loop as you think. He came by just last week over my case about a cop's suicide that didn't feel right to him. Man, your dad can rip a new one when he gets going." A pager went off through the phone. "Gotta go. I hate December. Holiday idiots. I'll call when the tox screens come back, but it'll be several weeks."

"Great," Mitch muttered as the phone went silent. By then, Emily might be dead. He had to figure out what the hell was going on before they could get to her, and keep his pants zipped in the meantime.

Even if it killed him.

Chapter Seven

Mitch's ringing cell phone jerked him out of a sound sleep. Morning sun tinged with pink flooded through the bedroom shutters. He rubbed his eyes with a groan. No way. He couldn't remember the last time he'd slept all night.

"Bradford," his voice croaked into the phone, hoarse with sleep.

"What do you think you're doing, Mitchell?"

The barking question cleared the fog. "Dad?"

"Taking off with a person of interest, not checking in while undercover? You trying to get yourself drummed out?"

Mitch groaned and sat up.

"Are you listening to me?"

He forced his mind back to his father's berating. "Of course." But Mitch was in no mood to hear a lecture. He could turn the tables just as well as his old man. "Has Tanner been talking to you?"

Paul Bradford was silent for a moment. *Gotcha, Dad.*

"I have my sources." He eased the words out slowly.

That hesitation told Mitch more than his father's words. "Did your mole tell you I'm investigating not only a dead girl who just gave birth and the missing baby, but also a punk who escaped from custody? I brought him down for trying to kidnap a *pregnant* teenager. He broke out of holding. Can you remember the last time that happened? And more to the point, why wouldn't Tanner be surprised by it?"

The squeak of his father's wheelchair sounded through the phone. "Dad, you okay?"

Papers rustled. "Who was guarding him?" His father had gone into cop mode, snapping orders like the sergeant he would always be. Mitch had missed that part of their relationship.

"I don't have that information." His mind whirled with possibilities. "I can find out."

"You do that. Then feed me the name."

"Just how involved are you?" Mitch started to worry. His dad was a good cop, but he had to accept his physical limitations.

"Keeping my fingers in the pot. Just because my legs don't work anymore, doesn't mean my experience isn't valuable. Even to my son," Paul snapped.

"I never said—"

"You didn't ask, either." His dad's voice had softened slightly, with just a hint of accusation, and a bit of hurt.

"You're freelancing." Mitch realized the new computer equipment in his dad's office had more purpose than surfing the latest social-networking websites. "With Denver PD?"

"Sometimes."

"You've gone private. Be careful, Dad. The last PI I knew got his head blown off."

"Perry was a drunk. I'm careful."

"But you're not on this case."

His dad was quiet for a moment. "Not at the moment. Not unless you need my help."

Mitch didn't want any of his family anywhere near this case, but if his dad had inside information, he couldn't afford not to ask. "What do you think of Dane Tanner?"

"Ex-Special Forces. The latest hotshot detective." Mitch

could almost see his dad's fingers steepling below his chin, as they always did when he considered a question. "Driven. Wants to bring down the criminals. In a bad way."

"Is he an honest cop? Did his name ever come up in anything...unusual?"

"Not in the way you think."

"Spill it, Dad. Give me something. If I trust him, and something happens to Emily—"

"She might've killed her husband, Mitch. The evidence—"

Mitch slowly did the stretching exercises Emily had prescribed. Easy, slow, not too much pain. "I don't buy it. She was almost killed twice. Someone's out to get her, and I'm going to find out who."

"She's staying with you." The disapproval in Dad's voice came through the phone loud and clear. "Not at your place, I hope."

"I'm not a fool, but someone broke into her house on my watch. I'm being careful. She has nowhere else to go." Mitch paused. "She wants her son back."

"I know that hits you hard, especially after what happened to Ian's little girl, but—"

"I believe in her."

His dad sighed. "Okay. I taught you to trust your gut, but remember, we've both been screwed. My faith put me in this chair. Your trust of Adam got you shot. We should've seen the signs. You keep your eyes and ears open. I'll be madder than a starving tick if you get yourself killed."

"Should I go to Tanner?"

"Keep him in the loop. Not enough to put anyone in danger, but enough that if he's dirty he'll hang himself. Keep your enemy closer than your ally, Mitch."

"You talking about Emily or Tanner?"

"Both."

"That's what I thought. I'll contact Tanner."

Mitch ended the call with a quick tap to the touch screen.

"Why would you communicate with the man who might be trying to kill me?"

Emily's voice came out of nowhere. She'd cracked open his door and peeked through the opening, a towel around her head and another wrapping her body. She obviously didn't care she was one tug away from being naked in front of him. Her face was flushed, but he couldn't tell whether it was from the hot tub, a hot shower or pure anger.

She stalked over to his bed. Probably the latter.

"We had an agreement, but you're a cop at heart, aren't you? I thought I could trust you."

The accusation dug deep. He couldn't deny his deception or his assignment. That was one of the reasons he wanted to call Tanner, to convince the man to give him some room to investigate. He couldn't decide if his boss had called his dad for information or to warn him in a roundabout way. Either way, he must focus on who was trying to kill Emily. The tip-toeing around would have to wait.

"Things have changed."

"Yes. They're worse."

"Look. I won't reveal where we're staying, but I want to know what he knows."

"You're making a mistake. Perry said not to trust the Denver PD."

"I'm a cop, and you're here with me." Mitch rose from the bed and stood toe-to-toe with her, a fingertip away from snapping the towel from around her and finishing what he should never have started last night. "Why is that, Emily? Why haven't you just run?"

"Maybe I should have." She turned away from him.

"Don't. Either you're here with me, or you're not, but don't question my integrity. I've said I'll keep you safe, and I will.

If I have one inkling Tanner is involved, I'll push him out of the loop."

His stomach churned at the argument. Every word was true, except that their entire relationship was based on his lies, and he could see no way out of it. He'd long passed the point of admitting the truth to her.

"I'm your last chance," he argued. "Who else are you going to go to?"

She bit out a harsh expletive she had to have heard on the streets she'd so carelessly explored, then spun away from him and headed back toward her bedroom.

He raced after her wearing only his sweats and stuck his foot out as she tried to slam the door on him.

"Trust me." Mitch tugged her close to him and lifted her chin. "We're not done. I don't have this figured out yet, but I have resources. And we have new information. We'll find someone who knows something." He twirled a strand of hair around his finger. "People talk, Emily. This thing has too many players for someone not to crack."

She gripped his arm. "Don't talk to the police. Please. Not yet."

Could he answer her without one more lie? "As long as I believe it's not safe."

"I don't know if that's good enough." She blew out a frustrated breath.

"It'll have to be." He paused and let his finger toy with the tucked corner of the towel. "Get dressed. I have an errand to run, and I want to show you the safe room before I go."

"You're leaving me?"

Mitch crossed his arms. "I'm not taking you out in the open. It's not safe. I won't be gone long. Call in sick to work, because you're not going anywhere predictable until we solve this thing. Then go through Perry's box. See if you recognize anything else."

"I've been through every slip of paper and item in that box. The wine storage facility is on Kalamath. The number Perry yelled—eighty-five—could be a locker number."

"Or the year. You're not a bad partner," Mitch said, with a slightly bemused smile and a heavy heart.

A small rose blush traveled from her full breasts now barely hidden by the white terry cloth. Her lips parted slightly as she smiled at him, and the desire in her eyes flared. "Let me come with you."

"No. It's for your own protection. You can use the computer to track down the business owners while I'm gone."

Her jaw tightened. Just as quickly, the heat between them turned arctic again. "Fine." She pressed the door, trying to close it.

Mitch didn't budge. He didn't like the look in her eyes. It reminded him of her expression when the car almost ran her down that first night. Satisfaction. Secret knowledge. He couldn't let himself forget she was dangerous. "Emily?"

"I'm getting dressed. I'll run your check. I've become good at research."

"Which is why I asked for your help. You'll wait for me? You won't do anything on your own?"

"Contrary to your opinion, I don't want to die. I have to live. For Joshua." She tried to close the door again. He didn't move. "What?"

"Promise?"

"I won't follow the lead on my own." She glared at him. "Can I get dressed now?"

He nodded and let her slam the door closed.

Whew. She was sexy when she was angry. Mitch went back to his bedroom. He needed some space, a break in the case and a cold shower. And not in that order. Once he could tell Emily the truth, nothing would stop him from having what they both wanted.

He'd take her in his arms and wouldn't let her go until they were both trembling, exhausted and satisfied. Dropping his sweats, Mitch stepped beneath the chilly water, his aroused body fighting for control.

If she'd let him touch her when she learned about his lies.

EMILY STARED OUT THE front door as Mitch left in a huge pickup. Where, he wouldn't say. She'd expected him to hide the keys to his brother's other vehicles, but he hadn't.

He should have.

She'd promised not to follow the wine-store lead. She hadn't promised not to leave if she had a reason. Quickly, she headed to the basement, through the high-tech gym that Mitch's brother had stocked with more equipment than her own clinic. She weaved past the elliptical toward a nondescript door, more like the entrance to a hot water heater closet than a super secret panic room.

She turned the knob to reveal a concrete barrier with an embedded keypad. She knew that she'd be found out at some point, but it didn't matter. She couldn't trust anyone. Perry had told her that. She believed the man who had died for her.

She tapped in the code Mitch had shown her and walked into the safe room. Stocked with enough supplies to last weeks, it didn't look like a bomb shelter, but essentially that's what Mitch's brother had created. The elaborate décor and survival supplies weren't what attracted her attention, though. She wanted the fully operational security cameras, and the very high-tech computer system. She walked into a small secondary room. Sure, she could've used the office laptop upstairs, but there were more interesting toys in this communications center.

She'd watched Mitch carefully when he'd powered off the system. She sat down and turned on the switches. After a light-speed boot-up, she used the same identification and password Mitch had provided upstairs. She was in. She typed in the wine-storage company's address into the county's database and waited for the information to run.

While the government's computers churned slowly, she let her gaze wander to a small screen Mitch had surreptitiously turned dark. She flicked the switch. The system booted up. Just as she thought. GPS. She hadn't done all that research over the last nine months for nothing.

A green dot appeared on a screen, moving toward downtown Denver. The internal GPS provided the location of all the vehicles. Four dots were sitting a few hundred feet from her. The fifth headed closer and closer to the Denver Police Department.

"Please, don't go there," she said softly to the dot.

The car turned on the street, only blocks away, then slowed to a stop in front of the Denver PD building.

"You lied to me," she whispered.

The faith that had been growing ever so slowly since she'd met Mitch cracked. She didn't want to believe he'd lied.

The computer in front of her beeped. She had a name.

She glanced back at the green indicator. Still stationary.

With a muttered curse, she grabbed one of the portable GPS trackers from the table, scribbled names and addresses on a slip of paper and headed upstairs. She'd find out once and for all if she could trust Mitch Bradford.

She snagged a set of keys off the wall of the kitchen and headed to the garage. If he didn't have a heck of an explanation… She paused. She wouldn't do anything.

She'd be on her own. Again. Like always. But this time, her heart would be shattered beyond repair.

MITCH KEPT THE ENGINE running as he waited in front of the police department. He wouldn't go in. He rounded the block and came to a stop just as Dane Tanner walked across the street.

Mitch rolled down the tinted window. "You wanted to see me."

Tanner peered behind him. "Where you headed?"

"The vacant lot down the street. My kids have football practice, and I have some questions for one of the players."

"Is your charge safe?"

"She's holed up."

Tanner hopped into the truck. "I don't want to be seen with you. Drive."

"What's going on?" Mitch pulled onto the street.

"Ghost's breakout. It was too easy. Nobody saw anything. The cameras in holding mysteriously had a glitch during the hour it happened."

"Glad you finally acknowledged it was an inside job. I was beginning to wonder."

"Thanks a lot," Tanner said. "I hate cops on the take more than anything. Nice to know you thought I was one of them."

"I've been burned. You know that. Adam showed me the ropes. Saved my life more than once."

"And cost you SWAT," Tanner said. "Drug money will do it every time."

The words made Mitch's stomach seize. He shouldn't be surprised Tanner might think he was finished, but it still hurt like hell.

"I hate this." The disgust in Tanner's voice mirrored Mitch's thoughts. "I've asked your dad for some outside help."

Mitch couldn't hide his shock. "Why him?"

"He does a lot of work for…one of our top consultants." Tanner shrugged. "Maybe you should ask him. Sounds like an internal communication problem to me."

Mitch bristled at the thought of his family keeping secrets. Then again, had he let any of them in on the true state of his rehab? He rubbed his thigh. They might be guessing, but they didn't know. Just like he couldn't be certain about Tanner. This entire conversation could be a setup. "What can you tell me?"

"Not much, but don't call my office line, Bradford. Only my cell. And keep *her* with you until I clear this up. I want whoever's messing with the Denver PD as much as I want Eric Wentworth's killer."

Mitch pulled up across from a large dirt field. A group of teens hovered at one end of the vacant lot. "I'll keep her safe." Then he stroked his chin. He decided to plant a seed. "Tanner? You see a missing person's report go through on a pregnant girl in the last few days?"

Tanner shook his head. "This that case you asked the guys to run?"

"Morgue got an ID through dental records. She'd recently delivered a baby. It's missing."

"You think it's connected to your case?"

"Do you like the coincidence?"

"Hell, no." Tanner climbed out of the pickup and rounded the vehicle. His breath puffed in the cold Colorado air. "Missing babies. Car bombs. This is bigger than we thought. Keep your charge out of sight. I don't know who's talking, but the perp's in the know." He zipped up his jacket. "I'll be in touch."

Dane started jogging back to the station. Mitch let the reality sink in. He had no backup. At least officially. If he got in trouble, he had few people he could call. Including his father.

"Hey, Coach!"

Ricky ran across the abandoned field. "You find Kayla?"

Mitch shook his head at the boy. "I checked out your sister, Ricky. Why didn't you tell me her boyfriend was arrested for assault? You holding out on me?"

GET 2 BOOKS

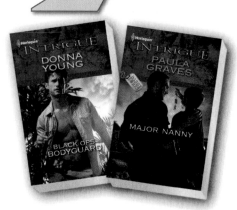

We'd like to send you two *Harlequin Intrigue*®
novels absolutely free. Accepting them puts you under
no obligation to purchase any more books.

HOW TO GET YOUR
2 FREE BOOKS AND 2 FREE GIFTS

1. Return the reply card today, and we'll send you two
   Harlequin Intrigue novels, absolutely free! We'll even
   pay the postage!

2. Accepting free books places you under no obligation
   to buy anything, ever. Whatever you decide, the free
   books and gifts are yours to keep, free!

3. We hope that after receiving your free books you'll
   want to remain a subscriber, but the choice is yours–
   to continue or cancel, any time at all!

EXTRA BONUS

**You'll also get two free mystery gifts!
(worth about $10)**

FREE!

Return this card today to get
2 FREE BOOKS and 2 FREE GIFTS!

Harlequin®
INTRIGUE

YES! Please send me 2 FREE *Harlequin Intrigue*® novels, and 2 FREE mystery gifts as well. I understand I am under no obligation to purchase anything, as explained on the back of this insert.

❑ I prefer the regular-print edition
182/382 HDL FMHU

❑ I prefer the larger-print edition
199/399 HDL FMHU

Please Print

FIRST NAME	LAST NAME

ADDRESS

APT.#	CITY

STATE/PROV.	ZIP/POSTAL CODE

Visit us at:
www.ReaderService.com

▼ DETACH AND MAIL CARD TODAY! ▼

H-I-03/12

If offer card is missing, write to: The Reader Service, P.O. Box 1867, Buffalo, NY 14240-1867 or visit www.ReaderService.com

BUSINESS REPLY MAIL
FIRST-CLASS MAIL   PERMIT NO. 717   BUFFALO, NY

POSTAGE WILL BE PAID BY ADDRESSEE

THE READER SERVICE
PO BOX 1867
BUFFALO NY 14240-9952

NO POSTAGE
NECESSARY
IF MAILED
IN THE
UNITED STATES

The boy looked down. "She wouldn't press charges. Stupid girls."

"You got any more little tidbits? If I'm going to help you—"

A black SUV pulled up behind Mitch's truck. A man stepped out of the car. "You owe me big, getting me out of a very comfortable situation in bed, if you get my drift," the man groused.

"Ricky, this is Ian. Ace football player. He's going to take my coaching duties on for a couple of days. Now, let's you and I talk." He turned to Ian. "You bring the equipment?"

Ian opened the back of his vehicle, revealing footballs, pads and more equipment than Mitch ever brought.

"You went overboard, but thanks, bud. I owe you."

"Yeah, you do. I swiped it from a local high school with the help of a very sweet English teacher who *was* going to make me breakfast."

"We'll return it, and I'll find a way to replace what got blown up yesterday."

Several boys shuffled over. Ian barked out a few orders and threw some balls to them. As they passed the ball around, Mitch rested his hand on Ricky's shoulder. "You know a girl named Vanessa Colby?"

"Sure." Ricky's face lightened. "Did you find her? She'll know where Kayla is. She's her best friend."

Chapter Eight

Nausea rose in Emily's throat as she approached the Denver PD building, but Mitch's truck wasn't there. She glanced at the portable GPS unit on the supple leather seat next to her. The blinking green dot indicated Mitch had parked his vehicle a few blocks away. She pressed down on the accelerator, her heart speeding up the closer she got.

She didn't know if she wanted to slap him or kick his injured leg. Okay, so she didn't want to really hurt him…or did she? Her heart felt empty, her entire being drained. She didn't want to believe he'd betrayed her. But the evidence… She didn't know how he could talk his way out of it. If he even cared enough to try.

Just ahead, she caught sight of his truck and an SUV parked behind it. She slowed a bit. The scene wasn't what she'd expected. Mitch stood with Ricky Foster, the teen whose sister had disappeared. Ian tossed a football around with some other boys in the vacant lot. She hesitated, but she'd seen the green dot parked in front of the Denver PD. She knew it. She deserved an explanation. She scooted in behind the second vehicle and stared out of the window. Mitch's narrowed gaze widened in recognition, then fury.

Before she'd even turned off the engine, he raced toward the SUV and yanked open the door, letting in a blast of cold. "What the hell are you doing here?"

Emily shoved him back and threw the portable GPS at him. "You lied to me. You went to the police. What are you, a spy? Undercover? Using me to prove I killed Eric?"

"I'm doing what I have to do." Mitch grabbed her arms. "They found a body. A blond-haired girl who'd recently given birth."

Emily gasped and shot a quick glance to Ricky, who caught a pass but then dropped the ball, clearly distracted.

"It wasn't Kayla," Mitch said. "It was her best friend. Seventeen years old."

Her anger flowed away. Guilt took over. "I thought—"

"Well, you should've waited until I got home. It's not safe—"

A shot rang out from the side of the street and pinged off the hood right next to Emily.

Mitch let out a shout at Ian and shoved Emily to the ground as the kids scattered. He draped his heavy body over her while she peered out from under him. Pounding footsteps slid to a stop next to them.

Ian crouched down.

"You see anyone?" Mitch asked.

"Shots coming from along the houses," Ian said in a clipped voice. "No visual on the shooter."

"What about the kids?" Emily panted as the rocks on the pavement bit into her back. She twisted just enough to see the once crowded lot now empty.

"Whoever it is, he's shooting at you, but the boys know what to do," Ian said grimly as he checked his .357. "A quick duck and disappear."

"Do all of your friends carry weapons?" Emily muttered, her knee digging into the pavement under her.

"Lucky for you," Ian said. "When you investigate dead bodies, you tend to question guys who carry knives and guns. A big gun keeps the lines of communication open."

"See if you can get a better view from behind my truck," Mitch ordered as he pulled out his cell phone and dialed for backup. After barking out the location, he pocketed his phone and shifted over Emily. She could barely breathe, and squirmed underneath him.

"Quit wiggling or you're going to get more than you bargained for."

She stared up at him as she felt his body harden. "How can you be thinking about—" her voice lowered to a whisper "—that when someone's trying to kill us."

"Stay behind the tire." He sent her a harsh glare. "I mean it."

Mitch rolled off of her, clearly keeping his body between her and the houses. Emily hunched over, trying to make herself as small a target as possible. Her lack of faith had put him in danger. This was all her fault. He peered around the front of the vehicle. Another shot rang out, and she heard the shattering of glass.

"Man, Noah is going to be livid," Mitch muttered. "The guy's a sucky shot unless he's just trying to pin us down."

"I can't see anything to pick him off," Ian called out.

Emily buried her head in her arms. She should've been more scared, but with Mitch here, she believed he'd get them out. She peeked up. Still placed between her and the shooter, he scanned the run-down houses across the street.

Another shot rang out, this time ricocheting off the front window.

"Ian," he called. "Get over here."

Within seconds, his friend was at his side. "He's behind a tree between those two houses," Mitch said. "I'm going in."

"You can't," Emily hissed. "Your leg."

He glared at her. "Do you want to get shot?"

"How about waiting for your SWAT buddies to get here?"

"I'm not waiting to be picked off like a carnival duck."

"Mitch…let me go," Ian said quietly.

"You haven't been trained for this. I have." Mitch gave a cocky grin. "Even with a gimpy leg, I've got one up on you, Ian. And you know it."

His friend paused for a moment, and Emily could tell he wanted to argue, but he finally nodded. She'd run into just enough of Mitch's stubborn streak to understand why.

"Protect her, Ian."

"I've got your back."

Emily shifted slightly, her heart pounding. Not for herself, but for Mitch. He serpentined from behind the truck. Two shots hit the ground behind him. She winced as his leg hitched about halfway across the yard, but he kept moving.

Four rapid shots fired. Then silence.

"Mitch! You there, bud? We clear?"

No sound. Emily's nails bit into her palm. Nothing but a siren coming toward them from the north. "Oh, God. He's hurt."

She tried to get up, but Ian shoved her down. "Don't. He wants you safe."

The intensity in Ian's gaze as he studied the houses made Emily shiver. He was afraid. "Mitch, you better shout out," he said, the sharp words the only thing that showed Ian's fear.

A sharp curse lit between the two houses. Mitch appeared in the yard.

Emily sagged against Ian's back. "Thank God."

"Perp took off," Mitch bit out when he reached them, dusting off his jeans. "He left his weapon. As he ran off, I noticed he wore gloves, so probably no prints. Hard to know if that was smarts or simply luck."

"Did you get a look?" Ian said.

"Dark hood, hidden face. Size and shape of Ghost, maybe, but it could've been anybody." He rubbed his leg and gave

Emily a solemn look. "I can't let you put yourself at risk like this again. You need someone who can really protect you."

She could see the intent clearly in his eyes. He was leaving her. He couldn't. Emily jumped to her feet and clutched his arm. "You can't do that. There's no one else I trust."

A black-and-white pulled up, followed by an SUV. Dane Tanner jumped out. He surveyed the scene. "Where'd the shots come from?"

"Long-barreled, scoped .22 semi-auto pistol over there." Mitch nodded toward the alley and then turned to Ian. "Get Emily into the truck," he said, pointing to the hulking, tinted-windowed vehicle. "I want as few people to see her as possible."

As Ian took her arm, Emily glanced at Mitch and Tanner. The detective looked back at her repeatedly. "Do you think he believes me?" she asked Ian.

"Mitch put his life on the line for you. How can you ask that?" Ian said.

"Not Mitch. Detective Tanner."

Ian opened the driver's side of the truck, and Emily slid in and over to the passenger's seat. "He's a tough one to read."

"Mitch hurt himself. I can tell by his gait," Emily said softly. "Because of me."

"You're a physical therapist. Help him."

"If he'll let me."

Ian let out a small laugh. "You already know Mitch well." He shot her a serious look. "Just don't let him down. He's one of the good guys." Ian closed the door and planted himself nearby, his stare alert.

Mitch shifted to his good leg. Maybe the best thing was for her to push him away, but how could she put Joshua's fate in the hands of anyone else in the Denver PD? Mitch Bradford was the only man who believed her, the only man she trusted.

Detective Tanner followed Mitch to the car and opened the door. "Are you okay, Mrs. Wentworth?"

"I'm fine. Mitch stopped him."

"I understand." Tanner faced Mitch. "I don't want to know where you're taking her, just keep her hidden." He turned his back. "Vance, keep those kids away from the crime scene," he ordered one of the flatfoots who'd responded.

Mitch eased into the vehicle.

"I saw that move as you ran across the street," Emily said. "Is your leg seizing up? I could—"

"Don't," Mitch said, turning toward her, his expression stone-faced. "You left the safe house. You followed me. You almost died. Again."

Emily couldn't deny the accusations. "If you'd only told me—"

"Don't put this on me, Emily. You're the one who left a fortress to wander around downtown Denver when you're a target." Mitch shoved the vehicle into gear and pulled away from the curb, studying the road behind him.

"You weren't honest," she muttered, knowing it was a lame excuse. She'd almost gotten them killed. She had gotten him hurt. Again.

The car jerked and his jaw clenched, but he said nothing. When he rounded two quick corners to confirm they weren't being followed, he sucked in a small breath.

He didn't know how long he could keep from rubbing his thigh, but he didn't want to give Emily the satisfaction or acknowledge how much that short, twenty-yard run across an uneven surface had brought the truth crashing down on him. He wasn't nearly where he needed to be to rejoin SWAT. He might never get there. And then where was he? A washed-up has-been, relegated to desk work.

"Why couldn't you tell me where you were going?"

Mitch slid her a sidelong glance. Her disappointment skewered him, and unfortunately he knew at some point she would feel the sting of his betrayal. "You have so much hope for the kids," he said. "Vanessa's story ended tragically. Kayla's probably will, as well. You didn't need that."

"I face a tragic reality every day, Mitch. Why would you still think I'm too weak to handle the truth?"

He shook his head. "You're one of the strongest people I've ever met. Don't doubt that. I just don't want to bring you any more hurt. Most of those kids will end up in places we don't want them to be."

"You still coach them. Following in your father's footsteps."

"Sometimes I don't know why. Dad's in a wheelchair because of that team. A punk my dad helped coach shot him while he was heading to practice. Severed his spinal cord. The boy got convicted but never admitted he did anything wrong. Never even said sorry." He turned to Emily. "It's why you have to be careful. You never know who'll turn on you."

"Were you coaching with him?"

"I was supposed to be there." Mitch stopped at a stoplight. Just the movement from gas to brake brought a wince of pain he tried to hide. Not as much pain as the truth, though. Still, he had to make Emily understand she had to guard her heart. Even against him. "He went alone, even though he knew the gangs had resurged into the neighborhood. Some of his kids were at risk. He just couldn't let it go."

"And now you're doing the same thing."

"That was *his* neighborhood growing up. He made his way out of it. He wanted other kids to have the same chance. He was betrayed, but I'm cautious." Mitch met Emily's gaze. "You can never be too careful."

Her blue eyes dripped with compassion. "He cared. So do you. That's not a weakness."

"You have to listen to me—"

"Yeah, not to care too much." She put her hand on his thigh, rubbing the ache there. "You care a lot." She eased her hand up his thigh just a bit. "I didn't believe in you today. I caused you to hurt. Let me help you now."

Mitch winced as sharp pains stabbed through him. She shifted her fingertips slightly, pressing hard against the knotting muscles. She released, kneaded again. One step at a time, one section after another she worked through the aching thigh muscle. The pain diminished into a dull ache as she pressed down in a particularly tender area just above his knee. Mitch let out a groan. That was the spot. "You have crazy-good hands."

"It's my job."

She worked through the trembling muscle fibers again. Mitch's hands eased on the steering wheel as the spasms and pain eased. She had magic fingers. Before the light turned green his leg felt almost normal.

"That's it," she whispered softly. "Ease up." She continued the massage. "You may not know it, but you are healing. If you relieve the strain and don't let it build, you'll mend even faster."

A car honked behind him.

Mitch pressed the gas. No pain.

"Better?"

"Thanks." Mitch hated he had to rely on her to get him through what should've been an easy chase, but this was his new reality. "I'm taking you straight back to Noah's. Then I'll call the owners of the wine-storage facility to let us in today."

"I tried already. No answer. It's Sunday."

"Try again," Mitch said, his voice harsh. Now that he no longer had the cramping and pain to focus on, he couldn't lose concentration on the slight vanilla of her lotion, the sexy sound of her husky voice or wishing those velvet hands would explore certain other parts of his body.

He adjusted in his seat to try to ease the pressure behind his zipper.

"Another cramp?" she asked as she pulled the slip of paper from her pocket.

"I'm good," he said. At her skeptical glance, he tried to smile without letting her see the want he knew flared in his eyes. "Promise. Just call."

Emily glanced down, and her cheeks flushed. She'd seen his arousal.

Squirming in her own seat, she dialed the number. "No answer. Again. Either home or business. They open at ten tomorrow morning, though."

"We get you to safety first," Mitch said. "Then regroup."

Emily was quiet for a moment. "I'm sorry I doubted you. I shouldn't have."

Yes, you should. Mitch wanted to scream the words, wanted to tell her the truth, but he knew better. Emily was just stubborn enough, just brave enough, to try to figure this out without help from him or anyone else in the police department.

He didn't speak, and she leaned toward him. "Can you forgive me?"

She whispered the words in his ear, her breath teasing his skin, making him shiver with awareness. Whether she intended the words to stroke him with sensuality or not, she'd awakened the fire burning just beneath the surface. He swallowed deeply as her unique scent wafted between them. He longed to touch her hair, turn her head to him for a kiss. His body tightened with arousal.

He sent her a sidelong glance. Her eyes widened, then flared in response to his need.

He could barely control himself before he waved at the

guard and accelerated toward Noah's drive. He pulled into the garage and switched off the key. The heat between them pulsed like an electrical storm. His pulse slammed against his throat. He should pull away from her, but he didn't want to. They were safe. They were alone.

Mitch unbuckled her seat belt and she scooted toward him, resting her hand on his chest. His heart thudded to meet her touch. He clasped her hand. "I won't stop this time," he said, his voice gruff. He looked at her, and she swallowed and licked her lips to wet them, begging for his kiss.

"I don't want you to."

"So be it." He opened his door and didn't say a word. He didn't have to. He pulled her out of the truck and slammed his mouth down onto hers.

Emily's head spun as he plundered her lips. Demanding, insistent, strong. He pressed against them, and she opened for him willingly, groaning as his tongue invaded her, tasted her.

His hands held her head steady as Emily snaked her arms around his waist. Her nipples tingled as her breasts pressed against his chest. She let her hands wander up and down his back, and he ground his hips against her.

"Give me what we've been wanting for the past two days," he said as he nipped her ear.

"Follow me." The husky words caught in her throat. She held out her hand, and he took it. She gave him her best come-hither look. "First one into the hot tub gets a massage."

Three steps and she stood in front of the door, waiting. Mitch pulled out the key, his smile more relaxed. "I've got the advantage."

"Perhaps." Emily eased toward him and let her fingertips toy with the waist of his jeans, releasing the button.

He sucked in his stomach and groaned. "You are a temptress."

Her lips pressed against the corner of his mouth. "No. I'm a woman who knows what I want."

She snagged the key from his hand and bolted through the front door, peeling off her clothes as she went. He followed, shucking his own. The muscles in his arms rippled as he tossed his shirt to the side. She wanted to memorize the lines and explore his hair-roughened chest all the way down to his narrow waist and beyond.

He obviously wanted her. He crossed the living room and grabbed her by the hips, pressing her against the wall. "I don't want the hot tub. I want you." His skin plastered against hers. She could feel every hard line of his body seeking hers out.

Mitch's lips lowered to her shoulder and he tasted her. "Mmm…you are so sweet, so sexy."

His leg pushed between hers, and Emily's body trembled. She'd never felt this kind of raw sensuality before. She wanted to shove him to the ground and take him, but she melted as he rocked against her, and an ache built deep inside her belly.

He pulled her closer, and her knees went to jelly. She clung to him. She wanted to be whole again, to be filled by a man who didn't keep secrets, who didn't hide from her.

She held him tight and rubbed her breasts against his chest. Her nipples beaded in response, begging for his caress. "Touch me." She leaned back, exposing her aching nipples to his gaze. "Kiss me."

He didn't deny them.

Still holding his body against hers, his hand traveled from her hip, past her waist and to cup her breast, kneading the soft flesh, teasing her.

Mitch grinned and kissed her cheek. "There?" His lips stroked her temple. "Or here?" Then he tested the corner of her mouth. "Or maybe here?"

Her mouth parted, and she tilted her lips to his, capturing him, her tongue tasting his, her hands holding his head to hers. A low rumble echoed in his chest. She couldn't get enough of him.

She grabbed his hands and took them to her breasts. "Here."

He lifted his head, and his smile vanished. He lowered his lips to her breast.

Her body soared as he wove his magic. She shivered and sighed against him. He lifted his head. "I want you."

She nodded, but she didn't stop touching him. She backed toward the bedrooms, and he followed, his arms still around her, his body pressing against her, then pulling away in rhythm with each step he took.

By the time the back of Emily's knees touched the bed, she could barely stand. She fell onto the mattress and tugged him to her.

Unwilling to wait, she opened her legs in greeting. Mitch looked down on her and groaned. "Protection?"

She flushed and shook her head, biting her lip in pure frustration. She wanted him. Now.

"This is my brother's house." He kissed her hard and rose from the bed and smiled at the view of her sprawled and waiting for him.

She knew her breathing was quick, her pulse pounding, her body ready for him.

"Stay right where you are. Don't move."

Her body hummed with anticipation, hungry for a touch, for release. What if he didn't find protection? There were ways to relieve the ache in their bodies, but she wanted him with her. She wanted him to be a part of her.

He walked through the door holding a large box.

"You expect we'll need all those?" she asked with a seductive smile.

"A man can dream." He stopped just inside the doorway

and stared at her. "*You* are my dream." Placing the box of condoms on the bedside table, he took a packet and stretched out beside her. "Help me," he said, his voice shaking slightly.

Her hands trembling, she touched him, and he surged in her hand before covering her with his body. He stared into her eyes as his hips flexed. She accepted him, and her body thrummed with joy as he filled her.

She let out a long sigh, and he smiled. He lowered his head to her throat and kissed her neck. Her scar.

She tensed under him as his mouth explored the ridge of skin at her throat that had so changed her life.

He raised his head. "You're beautiful."

"Don't kiss me there."

"You survived the attack." He moved his hips, and her world clouded over. "That makes you even more beautiful. I'll keep saying it until you believe it."

He drove into her again and again. The past melted away, and all she could feel was Mitch and his body as he worshipped her. He drove her higher and higher. His breathing grew ragged until finally she shuddered in completion.

When awareness returned, he was draped over her.

"Amazing," he whispered and kissed her throat once more.

Her hand reached to cover her scar, but he held it back. "Don't hide from me. You don't need to."

Tears burned behind her eyes at the intense satisfaction in his. She hadn't thought she'd ever feel this way again. Good. At peace. If only for a moment.

Her phone ringing stopped Mitch's caress from her throat toward her breasts.

"I don't want to move," she said.

"I'll get it." Mitch kissed the curve of her breast and rose, hurrying to find the phone tucked in her jacket pocket. "Blocked number," he said. "Sales call?"

Emily took the phone and pressed the screen. "Hello?"

"Mrs.…Mrs. Wentworth?" The whispering voice was urgent…and scared.

Emily's hand gripped the phone tight while Mitch's hand squeezed her shoulder. "Who is this?"

"It doesn't matter. But I wanted you to know. Your son is alive."

Chapter Nine

Emily's face went milk-white. She dropped the phone, and fear slammed through Mitch. He picked up the instrument and wrapped his free arm around her waist. "Who is this? What do you want?"

Emily grabbed the phone from him, her fingers digging into his skin. "Please. Tell me where he is. I'll do anything."

The desperation in her voice twisted his heart. Only one person on earth would evoke that kind of response in Emily: Joshua.

Mitch pressed his cheek against hers so he could hear the call.

"Who was that? Who's with you?" The woman's voice trembled to a barely audible whisper.

"A...a friend," Emily said, her voice shaking.

A shuddering breath escaped through the phone; then the slamming of a door sounded. "They're back. I'll call later. You get your son if I get enough money to escape them."

"I'll pay you anything!"

The phone went quiet, and Emily stared at it.

"She's gone." Emily tilted her head and met Mitch's gaze. "She said Joshua is alive. He's alive."

Mitch wrapped her close as she shivered uncontrollably against him. "Emily—"

"I know what you're thinking." She clutched at him even

harder. "That it's probably a hoax. But no one's ever called before. With everything happening to us, I have to take the call seriously. We've got to find out who she is."

He kissed her forehead. "Do you still have the tracer the cops put on your phone?"

Emily moaned, sagged back into the bed and covered her eyes. "They stopped it after six months."

Mitch gently removed her arm from her eyes. He took her hands in his. "We can find the number."

"I don't want the cops to know," she said. "I don't trust any of them."

Mitch couldn't stop the tension from entering his jaw. "Except me. And I have an alternative."

He grabbed his phone off the nightstand and dialed his dad's number.

"Mitch? You okay?" Paul Bradford's voice was deep with worry.

"Until Noah gets a look at his SUV," Mitch said drily. "Dad, I need your help. A blocked number traced. No cops. Can you do it?"

"Of course, but it'll take a bit of time if I don't go through the usual channels."

"It's more important to stay under the radar," Mitch said then rattled off Emily's cell number. "When can I have it?"

"Tomorrow?"

"Try to make it sooner. We may have a lead on Emily's son. If not, I want to nail the person who called."

The color drained from Emily's face, and Mitch ended the call before hugging her to him. "I'm sorry, but she could be playing you."

Emily shook her head. "I don't think so. She asked for money, but she really sounded afraid. I believe her."

Mitch leaned back against the pillows and folded her in his arms, tucking her under his chin. "We'll assume she's trying to get out of a bad situation. For now. I'll let Dad do whatever electronic voodoo he's been perfecting. Until then, we wait."

As he cradled her in his arms, Emily rested her head against his chest. He listened to her breathing and lay still, amazed this woman had wrapped herself around his heart. He wanted to tell her the truth, longed to wash the lies from between them. But she was proud and strong. Those things he loved about her made him afraid for her.

"I'm so glad you're the real deal, Mitch Bradford," she said, snuggling closer.

No, he could never tell her.

EMILY FELT WARM AND safe and protected, and he held her tightly, her back pressed against a strong chest. She wriggled against him, a pleasant soreness shifting through her legs and obvious desire pressing against her backside. He wanted her, even after they'd turned to each other twice more during the night. She felt better than she had in…forever.

Then she remembered.

She stiffened, her mind whirling. How could she feel this way when her son waited for her out there somewhere?

"Easy does it." Mitch's husky voice rumbled in her ear. "You're okay."

With a sigh, she faced the one man she could count on. She laid her hand against his cheek, his rough stubble scratching her palm. His hair was mussed, but his eyes were clear and concerned.

He drew a knuckle down her jaw. "What are you thinking?"

"That today could be the day I find Joshua."

Mitch sighed. "It might not pan out. I don't want you disappointed if she doesn't call back."

"I need the hope today. Last night was amazing. I'm glad I found you, but I want my son." Emily rested her head against his chest, taking comfort in the solid beating of his heart. "I was close to giving up," she said softly. "I never admitted it, never let myself say it out loud, but I was tired. Bone weary from all the disappointments. Then you rescued me." She rested her chin on her hands and stared up at him. "You gave me back the possibility. I needed someone in my corner. Someone who won't ever give up. Not until we've found him. You're that man."

His discomfort made her smile, and she kissed his chest. "Don't be embarrassed. I love that you don't back down or hide or avoid. You face challenges head-on. You're the only person in my life who's ever *really* fought for me."

A loud buzzing sounded from the bedside table, and Mitch sat up and flipped the alarm off. His awkward posture told her more than he'd ever admit aloud.

"I said too much," she said with a smile.

He looked over his shoulder, his expression sober. "I don't want to disappoint you," he said. "And I will."

She hugged his waist, laying her cheek against his back. "I don't believe that."

"You will."

He rose from the bed and slipped on his jeans. She took in his powerful shoulders, recognizing that once again he wanted to protect her. From hope, from being disappointed.

He was a good man, but he couldn't stop her feelings. Not about him, not about the phone call. This was the first news she'd ever received. There hadn't been a reward posted. She hadn't been in the papers or on television recently. She'd considered raising public awareness with an anniversary push to search for Joshua, but the Wentworths' latest accusations had squashed that opportunity. If she became more of a media target, Joshua would get lost in rumor and innuendo.

Mitch turned to her, his expression grave. "I have to go to the wine-storage unit."

"Take me with you."

He shook his head, and she gripped his arm. "I know you want to keep me safe, but we're not going to be out in the open. Besides, I can help you. I spent time with Perry. Maybe I'll recognize something."

He hesitated, then lightly kissed her cheek. "Bring your phone. If that woman calls again, put it on speaker. I want to hear exactly what she says." He drew her into his arms and tapped her on the backside as he kissed her lips. "Now go get dressed."

They pulled out of Noah's driveway in the truck a half hour later.

"At least it's not too far off the highway," Mitch said. "We should be there right as it opens. Gotta give Perry credit. Who would think of looking in a wine-storage facility? He was a whisky guy."

Emily studied the phone and checked again for a signal. "Why hasn't she called again?"

Mitch patted her leg. "Even if she doesn't, Perry was onto something. He died for what's in that locker. It'll give us a lead."

She nodded and stared out the window as they drove along the highway. Mitch, silent, threaded his fingers through hers. She glanced down, and warmth flowed through her veins. He was there for her, and for the first time in such a very long time, she felt like Joshua had a real chance. Her desperation and depression had given way to determination. This time, she would find Joshua. With Mitch at her side, she could do anything.

The drive seemed endless. When Mitch pulled across the street from the parking lot five minutes before the business opened its doors, Emily's heart skipped a beat.

He twisted in the soft leather seats. "Keep the phone with

you. Stay here while I check things out. We weren't followed, but I want to be sure you're protected."

"No one else has this information," she said.

"If there's one receipt, there could be more. I just want to be careful."

Mitch exited the vehicle, scanned the area and walked across the street. She could see the tension in his back, the awareness in his body. Like a mountain lion on the prowl. Without pause, he chose a path near a stand of trees. Momentarily, he stood strangely still, as if feeling for danger.

He searched the area, leaving no corner unexplored, even going so far as to place his hands on the hood of the cars in the parking lot. His every move filled Emily with confidence. He was wonderful.

He disappeared behind the building and a few minutes later came around the other side. In no time he rounded the truck and opened the door for Emily.

"Looks secure. No movement inside, but the owners could be in the office. The engines were cold." He glanced at his watch. "It's ten."

She stuffed the phone in her pocket, and they walked to the front door. He tugged on the metal handle.

It didn't budge.

"Locked?"

He rang the bell and waited another thirty seconds.

Still no response. Mitch peered through the window.

"I don't see anyone," he said.

A shudder of apprehension skittered up Emily's neck. She clasped Mitch's hand. His jaw throbbed, his entire body tense.

"Should we try another door?" she asked quietly.

Mitch banged on the glass. "I'm not leaving without checking this place out." He drew his weapon. "Stay behind me."

When he rounded the back corner, the pristine lot looked safe enough. Mitch walked up to a steel door. He tugged. It didn't budge. He didn't like the feel. Every instinct in his body thrummed with anticipation. His training told him to call for backup, but who could he trust? If the evidence was inside, how could he be certain it wouldn't disappear, and, with it, Emily's chance to find Joshua? Mitch never thought he'd come to a point where he'd completely turn his back on procedure. He'd live with the consequences.

If he found Joshua, it would be easy.

Mitch lifted a roll-up delivery door and let out a curse. Boxes were strewn everywhere. Wine bottles were broken. A bloody boot lay between two crates.

Emily gasped and followed Mitch as he walked toward the foot. A man lay on the concrete, his eyes wide open, a bullet hole in his chest.

"Stay close," Mitch whispered and knelt down. "He's cool to the touch. Been here awhile."

He rose and methodically searched the loading room, keeping constant watch on the entrances. Once he'd secured the area, he paused in front of a closed door leading into the main building. He turned to Emily. "Stay barricaded in here until I call for you. If you hear anything, anything at all, don't wait. Run. Take the truck and call 911."

"What about you?"

"This is my job, Emily. I can take care of myself, but Joshua won't have anyone if something happens to you. Understand me?"

She hesitated. "Mitch…"

He took her by the shoulders and forced her to meet his gaze. "Just promise me."

Emily bit her lip and nodded. He gave her a quick wink, slowly opened the door, slipped through and pulled it softly shut. A purring filtered through the quiet from his right. He scanned the room, and a cat's eyes glowed from beneath a table. The tabby was curled up against a woman's body, her face, arms and throat cut, a broken wine bottle at her side.

He rested his fingers against her carotid, but she had no pulse. A search of the rest of the building came up empty, and he hurried back to Emily, who stood poised in the door with a broken wine bottle for a weapon.

He wrapped his hand around hers and took the jagged glass from her. "Always the fighter." He led her into the shop. "Come this way."

He escorted her past the woman's body, but she paused, her hand covering her mouth, her expression shocked and saddened. "That poor woman."

"These guys don't leave witnesses alive."

"How'd they know about this place?"

"Perry's face was pretty bruised when we got there. They may have beat it out of him."

"Did they take his evidence?"

"We're about to find out." Mitch stood in front of wine-storage locker eighty-five. The gate hung at an angle. The lock had been forced open. "They ransacked the place."

Every bottle in the wine cabinet had been broken. The shelving torn apart.

Emily dropped to her knees. "It's gone. They destroyed everything."

Mitch knelt beside her and hugged her close. "Yes, they did." He turned her to him. "Which may mean they didn't find what they were looking for."

"But—"

"The woman's throat was cut with a broken bottle," he said. "Maybe they wanted information."

Her hand clutched at her throat.

"Might be the same people who attacked you, though they weren't very tidy."

"If they didn't find the evidence, where is it?" Emily asked. "Another compartment?"

"They destroyed the cabinet." Mitch stood and looked around the facility. There were numerous lockers, all numbered. "Perry said, eighty-five."

"That could've been the year of the wine, not the locker number."

"Maybe," Mitch mused. "Eight. Five. Eight times five. Forty. Eight minus five. Three. Fifty-eight." He walked along the corridor, scanning those lockers. Some were full; some nearly empty. "If we have to, we'll search them all."

"Eight plus five," Emily said, her voice tentative. "Thirteen. Mitch! Perry's lucky number was thirteen. He made a point of telling me this long, involved story of how everyone else's unlucky number was his rabbit's foot."

Emily's enthusiasm warmed Mitch's heart, but more than that, he'd come to recognize Perry had, at least in the last month of his life, laid some groundwork for them. "Did he share a lot of information like that story with you?"

"Not really. That's why it stuck out."

"Probably just what he intended," Mitch said.

They hurried over to locker thirteen. Inside were only three bottles of wine. He slipped on his gloves and forced open the lock. One more act that would get him suspended. Or fired. Right now, he didn't care.

He pulled the bottles one by one from the cabinet. "An eighty-five Merlot," he said. He hefted the bottle in his hands. "The weight is wrong."

He turned it over, studying it from every angle, then smiled. "Well done, Perry." He twisted the bottom, and it screwed open. A tube fell out. He opened the lid, revealing several sheets of paper coiled inside.

"Clever guy," Mitch said.

Emily started to remove the papers, and Mitch shook his

head. "No. Not here. Not now." He pulled out his phone and tapped the speed dial.

"Our fingerprints are all over this place. We have to be here when they arrive."

Emily gripped the tube. "You're not going to show them Perry's files?"

"Not yet, but you have to understand what we've done here today could cost us a prosecution."

"I want these guys in jail, but I won't let one more of Perry's clues get lost in the police department, Mitch. I only trust us to find Joshua."

Her words solidified the dark cloud on Mitch's soul, but he pushed it aside. "Let's get outside and wait for the cruiser. Then we'll go back to Noah's."

EMILY SAT HUDDLED IN the truck. Heat blared at her, and she clutched the wine bottle in her arms.

Cops swarmed the wine shop. Ian had shown up alongside the coroner. Two bodies in black bags had been carted off, and Emily hadn't ever seen Detective Tanner as furious as he was right now—or Mitch's expression as cold and withdrawn.

Tanner, his face red, pulled Mitch aside and poked at his chest. Mitch's entire body went stiff, and he reached under his jacket. He pulled out his gun and badge and shoved them at the detective, then turned his back on his boss.

Oh, no. She'd watched enough television to know what that meant.

Had she cost Mitch his job?

She needed his help, but she knew enough about Mitch to know his career meant everything to him. Otherwise he wouldn't be fighting so hard to get his SWAT position back. His work defined him. She couldn't let him sacrifice himself.

The weight of the bottle they'd hidden from the police

turned heavy. Maybe Perry had given her enough that she could help herself and Mitch at the same time. Once they found Joshua, everything would be fine.

She twisted the bottom of the bottle open and slid out the documents. She rifled through them, but at the top of one paper was a phone number and a single word circled: *Adoption.*

The word screamed through her head. She looked up at Mitch, who still argued with Tanner. She bit her lip and with a deep breath took out her cell phone and dialed the number.

Every ring vibrated through her, rattling her already shot nerves. She held her finger over the end call button. Another ring. Then a woman's voice came on.

"Anderson and Wiley. We specialize in private adoptions. How can I help you?"

She couldn't move. Couldn't speak. Had Joshua been adopted? Could this woman lead her to her son?

"Hello?"

Emily forced herself out of the fog. "Umm, yes. I wondered…I mean—"

"You're interested in adoption?"

The kind voice seemed like a grandmother's, and even though she wanted to spill out her entire story and scream at this woman to tell her everything, Emily hung on to the calm and patience she'd learned over the last year of dead end after dead end. Her mind whirled through possibilities, and she finally settled on a strategy.

"Y-yes. I don't really know what to ask."

"You want a baby."

"Oh, yes." Emily could hardly keep the eagerness from her voice. "I've tried so hard…"

"I understand, my dear. You have to know it can be expensive, though. Our young mothers need their living and hospital expenses paid, postpartum visits seen to, that sort of thing. I hate to be indelicate, but if that's not something—"

"Money's not an issue," Emily said quickly. When it came to Joshua, she would hock or sell everything she owned.

"Fine. If you'd like, we could set up a meeting with you. Discuss your options."

"I'd like that. When's your soonest opening? I really want—"

She knew the woman could hear her desperation, but she couldn't help it.

"I understand. It's an emotional issue. Tell you what. You sound like a nice girl. I could fit you in—" rustling paper filtered through the phone "—Thursday afternoon, I think. At the end of the day."

"I was hoping we could talk today." Emily couldn't hide the real disappointment.

"I'm sorry, dear. We just don't have time. If you're not interested…"

"Of course I am. I'll be there. Thank you. Thank you."

Emily secured the appointment, gave the woman a false name and ended the call. She leaned back in the seat, clutching the phone.

"What have you done?"

Mitch's deep voice nearly shot Emily out of her seat. The phone flew out of her hand. Standing just inside the open door of the truck, Mitch snagged the cell out of mid-air right before he tucked his badge and gun under his coat.

"You scared me." She glared.

"And you terrify me." He pressed a couple of buttons on the phone. "Who were you talking with?"

He crossed his arms and stood there, silent, waiting.

"I thought Tanner fired you," she said in a lame effort to change the subject.

He shook his head at the obvious attempt but answered

anyway. "He threatened to. I quit. He walked away in disgust with a lecture about protocol, then returned my badge and gun. We'll see."

Many might not be able to tell if Mitch was happy or not. His face was expressionless as stone, but Emily knew better. His voice was clipped and short as he toyed with the electronics in his hand, but the tension in his neck and arms told her he was furious.

"I'm glad," she said gamely. "I know your job means a lot to you."

"Give it a rest, Emily. Who did you call?"

She toyed with her too-long jeans. "You looked like you were in trouble. I thought maybe if I could find Joshua on my own, you wouldn't have to be involved…"

Mitch's gaze snapped to the open bottle and papers on her lap. He plucked them and scanned them. "You used one of the numbers?"

His jaw went tight, and his eyes flared with fury with a dangerous look that made her shiver. She'd seen it focused on others. She didn't like being on the receiving end.

He slipped into the truck and closed the door before twisting to her. "The adoption number?"

She nodded, avoiding his glance.

"What did you tell them?"

The softness in his voice made her shiver. There was not a whisper of the desire she'd experienced last night and this morning. He was a man trying to hang on to control.

"I just called to see whose number it was."

"I can hear the *but* in your voice. You didn't hang up, did you?"

She shook her head.

He let out a violent curse that made her wince. "Tell me every word that was said, and don't leave anything out."

As Emily relayed the conversation, Mitch released a tired

sigh and rested his head on the back of the seat. The more she spoke, the more and more she realized she'd been a fool. She was so used to doing everything on her own, working around the cops, that she hadn't considered anything but her own needs.

"Didn't it occur to you that I have contacts? You called from your phone. What if they track the number?"

"Perry made me block it, so my name doesn't show up."

"Thank God for small favors. That may give us some time, but if they forwarded your call to an 800 number, call blocking doesn't work. If they have contacts at the police or phone company, it's only a matter of time before they have your name."

So much she didn't know. She pressed her fingers to the bridge of her nose to try to ward off the headache threatening to pound behind her eyes while he drummed his fingers on the dash.

"Okay, first we cancel your phone."

"We can't. The woman could call again."

"Damn." Mitch rubbed his temple. "Okay. I'll make a couple of calls."

"I'm sorry. I didn't want you hurt because of me."

Mitch twisted in the seat and tucked her hair behind her ear. "You *have* to trust me, Emily. Let me help you. That's why I'm here."

She nodded. "I do trust you."

Her clear expression made his heart ache. For now, he just had to keep her safe. He would deal with the consequences— and there would be huge repercussions—later.

"How much trouble did I get us in?" she asked.

"I don't know. We'll deal with the fallout when we have to. For now, we take Perry's papers back to Noah's house and go through them. Then we plan our next move. *Together.* No more on your own. You got me?"

"Together."

Mitch yanked the car into gear and pulled into the street.

"Mitch," Emily said, her voice quiet. "I wanted you to know that it won't happen—"

"Hold that thought."

Mitch's knuckles tightened on the steering wheel. She recognized the intensity on his face. He checked both mirrors, reached the next light and, after it turned red, made a quick right. He let out another curse.

"You buckled up?" he asked.

Emily snapped her seat belt. "What's wrong?"

"We have a tail."

Chapter Ten

Mitch stepped on the accelerator and maneuvered through several sharp turns as Emily twisted and looked at the non-descript vehicle behind them. The SUV jostled her, and she gripped the door handle.

Mitch let out a long breath. "False alarm. This time."

Her gorgeous baby blues met his, concern filling them. He didn't like making her worry over nothing. He'd overreacted, but without the security of his department or teammates behind him, he couldn't afford to make any assumptions. No one had his back. Except Emily.

"Don't worry," he said. "I know how to prevent a tail. I'm not taking a chance on our safe house being compromised."

Mitch took detour after detour until finally Emily leaned her head against the seat. "Can we stop soon? Even I don't know how to get to Noah's house from here."

"That's too bad, because it's right around the corner."

"Thank goodness."

Mitch parked and bit back a grin as Emily leaped out of the truck. Nothing serpentine about her sprint to the house. He followed her in after she'd unlocked the house and caught her coming out of the bathroom, a relieved look on her face. "Remind me never to go on a long trip with you," she said.

"Some of us hack it, some of us don't."

"Some of us have abnormally strong kidneys." She smiled and sat down at the large dining table.

Mitch tugged a chair to her side. He'd seen enough of Perry's notes to know there were likely some leads, and to know they'd probably need help. Emily opened the tube and spread out the few sheets of paper the PI had stuffed into the hiding place.

Mitch turned the bottle over. "Pretty clever."

"Have you changed your mind about him?"

"Maybe. I still think some of those leads of his were totally bogus."

"Me, too."

He leaned back in his chair and stared at her. "My God. Emily Wentworth admitting someone was less than who they appeared to be. I'm stunned."

"I wanted to believe him. I try to give people the benefit of the doubt." She glared at him. "But I can see now that a lot of his early leads weren't…"

"Valid?" Mitch said. "I saw them. Missing children who were clearly custody disputes. He wasted valuable time."

"So did the police department. They kept investigating Eric and me. We weren't responsible."

Mitch couldn't fix the mistakes, but he could make a difference now. Only if she let him. He turned Emily's chair to him and placed his hands on her thighs. "Do you trust me? Do you trust that I have your best interests at heart?"

"Of course."

Mitch let out a slow, steady breath. He met and held her gaze. "Did you know your husband contacted Dane Tanner the day before the accident?"

"That's impossible." A slow dawning settled in her eyes. She sagged back in the chair. "Why didn't someone tell me?"

"I probably shouldn't have now, but I want you to think

hard, Emily. Remember the weeks before the accident. Did Eric act strangely? Did he do or say anything odd?"

She gripped his hands in hers.

All he could do was be there for her. He couldn't tell her what to remember, he could only try to pick apart the clues and uncover the truth. "I know it's hard, but the more we know about what happened that night, the better chance we have of putting these pieces together. Right now, things don't fit. An organized attack on you. Someone trying to frame you. Missing evidence." He ticked through the list, the implications becoming clearer and clearer. "Then the murders of Vanessa, Perry and the wine-storage couple. It doesn't track."

Emily pulled her hand from his, and the loss of her touch tore at Mitch's heart, but not nearly as much as the heartbroken look on her face.

"I've been thinking about Eric a lot the past few days," she said. "He was a wonderful man, but he wasn't perfect. He pulled away from me the last couple of months of my pregnancy. He wouldn't talk to me. There were whispered conversations over the phone. At the time, I wondered if he was having an affair." Emily wrapped her arms about herself. "I've never said those words aloud. Not to anyone."

Mitch wouldn't let her fold back into herself. He clasped her hands lightly in his, stroking the pulse point at her wrist with his thumb. "What do you believe now?"

She stared at the floor and finally raised her head, her expression haunted. "I think he knew we were in danger. I don't know why or how, because money was tight, but I think he set up that account with money so we could run away if we had to. He just didn't tell me. He wasn't honest." She squeezed his hands so hard her fingers turned white with the effort. "Can I forgive him for that?"

The despair in her eyes made him hurt for her, and he shivered in apprehension for the future he'd recognized he wanted with Emily. Every hour that passed made him doubt it would ever happen.

"Did he say anything after the accident?"

"Not that I remember, but the whole thing is still bits and pieces. Flashes of a red and green tattoo, the bloody blue blanket, a hooded man. It's all mixed up in my head."

"That's why you wanted to see Ghost's tattoo." The request made sense now.

"I thought it might jog my memory. Perry agreed."

"It's all coming back to Perry," Mitch mused as he aligned the papers side by side.

"He was a good man," Emily said. "In spite of his mistakes."

Mitch smiled at her. "That's what I lo…like about you. No matter how much evidence you see, you still have faith."

Had he almost said *love?* Oh, God. He couldn't feel that way. Not with his deception still between them. He cleared his throat and leaned down to focus on the papers. "Besides the phone number, he has some notes. Too bad they're so random."

"I guess it was just too much to hope that we'd get an address for Joshua," Emily sighed.

"Well, well, well." Mitch looked at the circled words. *Tattoo—not Ghost. Florida.*

"Wait a minute," Emily muttered. She ran from the table into the bedroom and came back with Perry's box. She dug into it and pulled out a slip of paper. "Perry followed someone down to Florida."

Mitch turned one of the sheets over. "Here's something else. *Florida. Airline. December.* One year ago."

Emily's eyes widened. "Is Joshua in Florida? Did Perry know where Joshua was and not tell me?" She rose from the table and started pacing. "I know he wasn't perfect, but he knew what that information would mean to me."

"Maybe that's why he wanted to be sure."

Mitch couldn't believe he'd defended the less-than-stellar PI, but he understood the man's desire to protect Emily from any more disappointments. Mitch scanned the next spattering of notes. "*Cop. On the payroll. Without more, that's no help.*" He flipped the paper over. "*Marie.*"

Emily peered at the notes. "What? A cop named Marie?"

"Marie is a midwife. And, according to Perry, a murder witness."

Emily pulled the phone from her pocket. "Do you think Marie is the woman who called?"

"There are no other names on this sheet of paper. And Perry's death made the news."

"She knew Perry."

"And she's probably helping deliver young girls' babies," Mitch said, his voice grim. "Perhaps she knows where Kayla is."

"But what about Joshua?"

"I still don't understand that connection. Joshua was taken well after he was born."

Mitch's pulse pounded, the adrenaline rush not much different than when he waited to bust through a door with a battering ram. Strange how a few pieces fitting into a puzzle could get him going. He nabbed his phone. "I'm calling Dad. He can probably use this information to speed up his search. Besides, I need more. I need to find a woman named Marie who's a midwife in Colorado *and* how many baby boys were adopted in Florida in the last year."

Emily tucked her legs underneath her as he made the call. He gripped her hand in his as he provided his father the latest information. Mitch already had a plan in mind. "I need a way to travel fast if something breaks," he said into the phone.

Once he'd hung up, he framed Emily's cheeks with his hands. "He'll find her."

Emily leaned into him and wrapped her arms around his waist. "Do you think we'll find Joshua?" she asked.

Mitch hugged her close. "We have a chance."

THE MORNING SUN FILTERED through the shutters. Emily watched the light dancing on the walls as she rested her head against Mitch's chest. She hadn't been able to sleep. He'd asked her to work his leg, but he'd just been trying to distract her. He'd done more than that. She let her hand wander over his bare chest, memorizing the feel of him, the light dusting of hair on his chest. He was so strong, so confident about everything. He'd even become more accepting of his leg's limitations.

Though a few well-placed caresses had helped that along.

She padded across the room and slipped into the clothes she'd borrowed. The phone was heavy in her hip pocket. No one had called either one of them since Mitch had spoken to his father.

Why didn't Marie call back?

After a quick stretch to work out the kinks, she made a cup of tea in the hardly used gourmet kitchen and settled into the corner of an overstuffed sofa in the living room. The dancing lights over the unusual view of Mitch's brother's interior jungle pool soothed her like a fine massage. She felt safe here. There were cameras, motion detectors, a sophisticated alarm system tied directly to the cops.

Emily just had to be careful not to activate it.

A slight clicking of the side door's lock made her tense. It opened slowly. Emily didn't hesitate. She opened her bag and pulled out the gun he'd given her from Noah's collection.

A bearded man in straggly clothes stumbled through the door.

Emily raised the weapon. "Don't move or you're dead."

The bum approached her, a duffel on his back. His head

tilted to one side as if he were trying to figure her out. *Great, just great.*

"Mitch!"

"You don't belong here," the deep voice muttered from behind the beard. He walked forward two paces.

Her finger tightened on the trigger. "Stop. Or I shoot."

He stilled.

Emily felt warm breath on her cheek.

"Mitch," she whispered.

"Nice girlfriend, little brother. Knows you just by feel. Since you're naked as a jaybird, I guess you two are together."

"Give me the gun, honey. I know you want to shoot him, but the flea-ridden carcass is Noah. Denver's most eligible bachelor, geek first-class, filthy rich and the world's most annoying older brother."

Mitch slipped his palm over the weapon, and she released the gun to him. He disappeared from behind her, hopefully to put some pants over that fabulous body of his, though she couldn't resist sneaking a peak at his very appealing backside as he walked away.

The man winked, and she felt the heat creep up her cheeks. Despite all his magazine covers as a tech whiz, she wouldn't have recognized him, though his eyes were definitely familiar. Noah Bradford had Mitch's eyes.

He crossed the room and held out his hand. "You *really* would've shot me?"

"No question."

"I like that in a woman."

Though his lips tilted up at the corner, the smile didn't reach his eyes. The dark pupils held shadows and a dangerous glint that Emily had only seen a few times in Mitch. Noah, however, had that expression even when he tried to grin. Mitch's family just grew more and more fascinating.

"But you hesitated too long," he said. "If I'd wanted to, I could've eliminated the threat."

"Why didn't you?"

"I like petite spitfires with gorgeous long, silky hair," he purred, sidling up to her.

"Watch yourself, bro," Mitch growled. "You have hundreds of women flocking to your bed. Bizarre, considering you make your living behind a computer monitor. Leave mine alone."

Noah threw up his hands and backed away. "Just seeing where you stand, little brother."

Emily shivered at the possessive statement. Normally she would've been irritated by such macho posturing, but she appreciated the brothers' dynamic. They were family. She missed that. So much.

"Thanks for coming so fast."

Mitch hugged his brother in one of those bear hugs that made Emily smile. There was caring there, and love and trust. Family.

"Seems like old times," Noah said. "Bailing you out of another mess, except you usually don't get my car shot up."

"Dad ratted me out, didn't he?"

"Actually, the cops called since it's *my* SUV."

"I'll pay to have it fixed," Mitch said. "Speaking of Dad, we're going to have a few words after this is all over about the high-tech investigation he's into these days."

"I was going to tell you—"

"You'll tell Chase and Sierra, too. Dad might be moving too fast. You ever think of that?"

The Bradford brothers clearly didn't mind a little conflict. So different from her family, and so very different from the Wentworths. William and Eric both avoided confrontation to the point where they turned inward. Strange how she noticed the flaw so much more now that Mitch had entered her life.

"Did the rest of you consider how you've discounted his abilities since he lost the use of his legs?" Noah challenged.

"He needs to take care of himself first."

"So, I guess that means your investigation should just be desk duty, bro. Let me fund someone who can take over. I know about your leg. It's seventy-five percent, and that's being generous."

Mitch didn't attack his brother. He simply stilled. "Touché, Noah."

Emily stepped between the brothers. She stood toe-to-toe with Noah and stared up at him. She couldn't care less that his six-foot-four-inch frame dwarfed her. "Are you a doctor? Because unless I see an M.D. after your name, you have no business judging his capability. I, on the other hand, as a physical therapist, know exactly the extent of his recovery. In any case, I've gotten closer to finding my son in a couple of days than the entire last year. And it's because of Mitch, so lay off."

Noah took a step back and raised his hands. "I surrender." He shot Mitch an amused glance, which made Emily's hackles rise even further. "Passionate little thing, isn't she?"

Mitch smiled. "You have no idea."

"I'm standing right here," Emily said. "Why don't you make yourself useful? Help us instead of attacking the man who's gotten me closer to locating my son than the entire Denver PD and FBI?"

A blush colored Noah's cheeks above his beard. "Sorry," he muttered. "Noah's taxi service at the ready. When do you want to leave, ma'am?"

Mitch snagged a notebook from the table. "Last night Dad narrowed the list to a few Florida families who took custody of baby boys the month following Joshua's disappearance. We'll start there."

"We're going to Florida? Now?" Emily said, her jaw dropping.

"As soon as you're ready. Noah's flying."

Noah picked up his duffel. "You calling the cops?"

"No!" Emily and Mitch yelled at the same time.

"Okay." His gaze narrowed. "Is that why you've got Dad running these crazy searches and keeping such a low profile?"

"There's an informant—maybe more than one—at the police department. I'm not taking chances. If they learn where we're going—"

"I could lose my only chance to find my son," Emily finished. "We can't trust them."

Noah's gaze had gone solemn. "Got it. We leave low-key." He rubbed his beard. "I was—out of pocket—but I think I'll keep this for now. Less chance of me being recognized. Give me fifteen minutes to shower and change. Can you be ready?"

"I've been prepared for this moment for a year," Emily said.

Noah disappeared down a hallway toward the master bedroom. Emily turned to Mitch. "When did you call him? You didn't tell me about it. Another secret, Mitch?"

"You were showering after last night's first round of… exercise. Luckily, he was in the country." Mitch cupped her face in his and lowered his lips to hover over hers. "This is a long shot. You know that."

She twisted under his arms and faced him. "Don't try to kiss your way out of this. I thought we had an agreement. You're keeping me out of the loop on the best chance we have."

"To stop you from doing anything crazy," he muttered under his breath.

She bristled, and he cleared his throat. "Look, we know Marie went to Perry. But we still aren't sure if she's credible.

She hasn't called back. If that was even Marie on the phone in the first place. I'm trying to protect you. I just don't want you disappointed."

She sucked in a deep breath. "It's the best chance I've ever had, Mitch. Don't leave me in the dark. I've been there for too long."

He hugged her close, resting his chin on the top of her head, and she settled against him, drawing strength. "I need you to believe in the possibility right now. Please. No pessimistic, cop attitude. Just be the man in my life who believes in me, who is honest with me, who is my partner."

He kissed the top of her head. "I'm in your corner, Emily. Always."

MITCH SLID HIS LONG shirtsleeves up. A drop of sweat trickled down his back as he hunkered in the rental car. "Eighty degrees in December is just plain wrong. Give me Colorado's snow and cold over Orlando, Florida, any day. I like winter."

Emily had tucked her knees up under her chin as she stared at the house across the street. Her face was tense, wary, her optimism fading after so many hours.

He slid his hand on top of hers. He wanted everything to work out, but there were so many missing pieces, too many unanswered questions. Even if they found Joshua, Emily would still be in danger. For now, he had to keep her spirits from sinking after the high hopes she'd had. "We still have a chance."

"I thought we'd come down here and just find him. It would finally be easy."

They'd peeked into the window of the first address. Recent photos had decorated the walls. The baby had been of African-American descent.

Noah hadn't had any better luck in Jacksonville. His quarry had had red hair and freckles. Even looking scruffy, the man had charmed the kid's mother in the park, getting her to show him the boy's baby photo. No resemblance to Joshua.

"We still have two more possibilities. Noah hasn't called yet about his second family."

"Maybe we're in the wrong place," she said. "Maybe Marie lied."

"Where's that faith you wanted me to give you?"

"I'm running on empty, Mitch. What if he's not in Florida at all? What if Marie is just some sick person who wanted to hurt me? Maybe one of Victoria's friends playing a cruel joke…"

"Then we've had a ride in Noah's Citation, and we regroup. We take advantage of the appointment you made at the adoption agency." Mitch kissed her. "We don't give up. You taught me that."

Mitch's phone rang, and he pressed the speakerphone. "Noah. What you got, man?"

"Sorry. It's not him. This little boy has dark hair, so I was doubtful, but these people are his aunt and uncle. His parents were killed in a car accident, and they adopted him."

"Thanks. You heading back this way?"

"I'll be ready to take everybody home when you're finished there."

Emily's fallen expression nearly broke Mitch's heart. She bowed her head and pressed her eyes against her tucked-up knees. His hand reached over and kneaded the back of her neck. "We still have this house. It's not over yet."

She sighed and tilted her head toward him. "This is the last chance."

"You're wrong. Perry gave us more than this lead. We have the phone number to the adoption agency. With Dad's help and Noah's taxi service, we have options."

Emily took a shuddering breath. "Right. Options."

Her eyes tracked to an SUV coming toward them. The vehicle pulled into the driveway and Mitch checked the license plate against his list.

"Jim and Judy Greenley."

Emily started to open the door.

"Not yet. No ambush. Let's take it slow. I don't want to scare them into calling the local cops. We still don't know who the mole at the Denver PD is."

Emily bit her lip. She nodded when Mitch's phone blared in the quiet car.

"That can't be Noah." He glanced at the caller ID. "Tanner. Damn." Mitch shoved the phone back into his pocket. "Not a distraction I need right now, since he doesn't know we left Colorado."

Emily's phone rang. She jumped, then scanned the screen. "Tanner must really want to talk to us."

"If it were news, Dad would've let me or Noah in on it. I'd rather return Tanner's call after we find Joshua and are back in Colorado."

Mitch studied the scene from where they'd parked. A man opened the front door and reached into the back, pulling a squirming baby out of a car seat. The flash of light brown hair looked promising; the blue shirt and denim overalls screamed *boy*.

Emily gripped the age-enhanced photo in her fingers. "He could be Joshua," she said. "His hair is the color of Eric's."

"And yours," Mitch said, letting the silky strands slip through his fingertips.

A woman exited the passenger side, and the small child reached for her. She laughed and took the boy, cuddling him to her.

"They look happy," Emily said, her voice solemn. "They look like a family."

"Yes, they do."

She gripped Mitch's hand. "What do I say?"

He stared into her eyes. "You tell them the truth."

"It's been so long. Joshua won't know me. What if he cries? I don't know if I can handle his tears."

"He might not know you at first." Emily's eyes glistened with tears, and Mitch kissed her. "But he'll recognize your love, Emily." Mitch held out his hand, and Emily placed her small one in his. "You can do this."

The walk across the street seemed like miles. Step after step. Emily hesitated. He didn't blame her. If the Greenleys didn't have Joshua, they were back to hoping Marie called again. The woman was another *ghost*.

They walked up the driveway toward the couple, who stopped, their faces curious.

Jim Greenley stepped forward, his stance curious but protective. "May I help you?"

Mitch pulled out his badge. "Mitch Bradford, Denver Police Department. Could we ask you a couple of questions, Mr. Greenley?"

Emily didn't move. She simply stared at the small boy toying with his mother's blond hair.

All Mitch could make out was the color of the boy's hair. He seemed healthy. He let out a joyful giggle as his mother tickled him. "Your son seems happy," Mitch said quietly.

The man preened with pride. "A chip off the old block. Now, Officer. What can I do for you."

At the sound of his father's voice, the boy turned and reached out his arms. "Da!"

His upper lip had a scar. A very identifiable scar. This child had had a cleft lip repaired.

He couldn't be Joshua.

Chapter Eleven

Emily sagged against Mitch as she stared at the baby's mouth.

"Do you have a problem?" Jim Greenley snapped. He folded his arms across his chest.

The man's combative stance made Emily realize she was staring at the boy. She forced herself to face the increasingly hostile parents. "I'm sorry. Your son is about the same age as mine."

Judy Greenley relaxed, then smiled. "Oh, is he with you?"

The words sliced through Emily as the truth took hold. She bit her lip to stop it from trembling. She couldn't get the words out.

Mitch stepped forward, tucking her closer. She needed him. So much.

"Emily's son was stolen when he was a month old. We have reason to believe that he was adopted here in Florida."

"You can't think…" Judy's hold on her son tightened.

Emily recognized the fear on her face.

"No, ma'am. Emily's son didn't have a cleft lip.

Judy let out a deep sigh.

Emily wanted nothing more than to get out of there. She stepped backward, but Mitch held her fast next to him.

"Your son is adopted, isn't he?"

Jim Greenley's expression grew suspicious.

"Please," Emily said. "We're just trying to find my son,

and we're not familiar with this area. It would save so much time."

The man's face softened. "He's ours. Everything above-board. We went through a well-known agency."

"I understand," Mitch said. "Would you mind giving us the name?"

"Sommerfield Adoption Agency. They're based here in Orlando." Jim Greenley pulled his wife into his protective embrace. "They have a good reputation," he reiterated, as if he were trying to convince himself.

"I'm sure they do," Mitch said. "Thank you for your help."

Sommerfield? That wasn't the name on Perry's notes. Was this all a wild-goose chase? Renewed fear shook her, but Mitch propped her up, standing strong next to her.

"I hope you find your son," Judy Greenley said softly, cradling her boy.

"Thank you. Enjoy your boy. He's a gift."

Emily's eyes burned with unshed tears. Their last lead was gone.

Mitch turned her away and whispered in her ear, "All we have to do is make it to the car."

She nodded and stumbled beside him to the street. She couldn't think, couldn't feel. Her entire body had gone numb with disbelief. No matter what she'd said as each disappointment had occurred over the last several hours, she'd never believed they'd fail.

She stared up at him, his face blurry through her tears. "I don't know where my son is. I don't even know where to look."

"Let's get you in the car," he said.

A black-and-white tore down the street at them. Mitch shoved her toward the SUV. "I shouldn't have used my credit card at the rental company. Get inside."

The police car skidded to a stop right next to him as the

stunned Greenleys looked on. Jim pushed his family inside their house just as a young cop slammed his door, his hand on his weapon. "Officer Bradford?"

Emily eased toward the SUV. "Please don't move, ma'am. Keep your hands visible."

"No sudden movements, Emily," Mitch said softly.

She stilled next to the rental, and he took a deep breath. "What's this all about?"

"Detective Dane Tanner asked me to find you. He needs to talk to you. Immediately."

"What the hell for? And how did you know where we were?"

"Rental car GPS. Um…the detective instructed me if you resisted, I should bring you in for questioning. In handcuffs." The young officer pulled out his notebook. "You're still conducting surveillance on a—Emily Wentworth?"

Oh, God. Surveillance. The word echoed around in Emily's head. Her knees shook. No. It couldn't be true. It just couldn't. She had to steady herself on the hot metal of the SUV. Not Mitch. Please, not Mitch.

His head whipped around toward her, and she could tell by the guilty expression on his face. It was true. He'd used her. He hadn't believed in her. Ever. He'd just been doing his job.

Everything that had happened between them…. She'd— oh, God. She'd given herself to him. She'd let him inside her heart. She'd thought she might even…love him.

What a fool. "You bastard," she said.

The cop wiped his brow. "I screwed up, didn't I?"

Mitch blew out a long hiss of air. "No, kid. I did." He pulled out his phone, walked away from them and placed the call.

Emily watched him, the man she'd thought she knew.

When he returned, she glared at him. "Are you planning to arrest me?"

"Of course not. I—"

"Save it, Mitch. Just get me out of here so I can catch a flight home."

"Noah can fly—"

"I don't need your help. Or your family's." She crossed her arms and planted herself solidly. "Don't try to talk your way out of this, *Officer* Bradford. You had plenty of time to tell me. In bed and out."

The young cop's jaw had dropped, but he listened unabashedly, and she didn't care.

"I know you're upset, Emily," Mitch said, his voice lowering to a whisper. "I don't blame you, but I did what I had to do—"

"To put me in jail."

Mitch thrust his hand through his hair. "Can you just listen for a minute? I did it all to protect you. It didn't take long to understand you were in trouble. I knew if you found out—"

"Oh, so it was inconvenient to tell me the truth. I told you what Eric did, and still you said nothing." She faced him, anger pouring from her, all the while disillusionment sucking the life from her soul. "You couldn't have hurt me more. How can I trust you again? With the truth? With my fears? With my heart? With my son?"

He paled, but she wasn't in the mood to sympathize. She hoped and prayed someday he would feel the pain that shot through her heart.

"I can only tell you that everything I did was for you. And for Joshua," he said quietly.

"How can I believe that? Your job was to prove I killed Eric, wasn't it? I've probably given you enough circumstantial evidence to tie a bow around a conviction. You can become the big hero. Get back your job with SWAT." Her entire being froze from the inside, despite the hot, muggy weather. "I want you out of my life. I don't want you or any other Denver police officer anywhere near me. Got it? I'll find Joshua on my own."

"You can't do this alone. You're still at risk. That's why Tanner called. They found a woman's body in the foothills of the Rockies. Not too far from your house."

Emily's heart skipped a beat. "Kayla?"

"No. An older woman."

The words shattered the last fragment of hope in Emily's chest. "Marie?"

He nodded. "Marie Dumond. She had a cell phone, and yours was the last number she dialed."

AFTER RECOGNIZING SHE couldn't afford to get back to Denver any other way, Emily succumbed to Noah's cajoling and agreed to fly home with the Bradford brothers. She couldn't think as Noah escorted her onto his CJ4 jet. She'd fully expected to have Joshua on the way up these steps. Now her arms were empty, and so was her heart. The one lead she'd counted on—Marie—was silenced forever. Her gullibility and stupidity were clear for everyone to see.

She'd believed Mitch had her back when they'd arrived in Florida even though she'd wondered about him in the beginning. Just like she'd suspected Eric. Why had she refused to listen to her instincts instead of believing what her mind wanted to be true?

She ducked into the cabin and sat near the rear, as far away from the cockpit as possible.

Mitch followed. He'd handled the steps well. Not that she cared, of course. Not her problem anymore.

He hesitated beside her seat, as if wanting to say something.

"This seat's taken." She placed her purse down and gave him the best glare she could.

"Fine. I'll sit up front with Noah."

Mitch snaked into the copilot's seat, and Emily let out a relieved sigh. Noah made the last checks around the plane and locked them in. He knelt beside Emily. "Mitch didn't want to lie to you."

"But he did. I can't trust him."

"And you won't stop until you find your son, will you?"

"No."

Noah patted her leg. "Let me have your cell."

"Why should I?"

"Because I'm one of the good guys." Noah gave her a cocky grin so like Mitch's it made her belly ache.

Hesitantly she dug into her pocket and handed him the device. He snagged a small tool from his back pocket and with a couple of twists opened the phone to reveal its guts. After a few deft movements, he closed the phone and returned it to her.

"I took out the GPS and put a handy little gadget in that will block your number, no matter who you call. Just to be safe."

"Who are you?"

"Just your standard, ordinary computer jockey," he said, flashing a charming smile.

"Right. Just like Mitch really cared about me."

Noah's smile vanished. "No, Emily. Mitch cares. A lot." Noah rubbed his beard. "You pulled a gun on me back at my house. You know how to use a .40 Glock?"

"My private investigator taught me how to shoot. He thought I might need the training." Poor Perry. He'd been right more often than Mitch or the police department had ever believed.

Noah opened up a small compartment over her head and handed her a large pistol and a clip. "It has a big kick, but it'll stop most anything or anyone. If you're going to try to investigate on your own, you're going to need it. Just don't use it to kill my brother. Even if he's an idiot, I'm fond of him. Dad would be disappointed if I provided the weapon that sent Mitch to the pearly gates."

Emily accepted the weapon. "Thank you."

Noah sighed and looked over his shoulder. "I think he loves you," he said and disappeared into the cockpit.

"No, I'm just a job," she whispered. She had to remember that.

"Buckle up." Noah's voice filtered through the intercom system.

Emily snapped on her seat belt and leaned back, gripping the weapon in her lap. Mitch's betrayal stung, but it didn't change her mission. With Mitch untrustworthy, Perry gone and Marie dead, she had one more option that she'd forgotten about until just now. She would keep the appointment with the adoption attorney. It was a long shot, but it was all she had.

For the next four hours, Emily went over every scenario she could think of. Mitch had tried to talk to her several times. She shut him down. She needed help, but not his. Not again. She thought about asking Ian, but she couldn't allow herself to use Mitch's best friend. He was a single parent with a young child. That meant going back to William. Trying to convince him to help her find another PI, and to pay for it until the house sold. Not an easy task in this market. Even more so considering her house wasn't safe with these people after her.

She didn't have a place to stay, either. Or a car.

Noah announced their approach to Denver, and Emily braced herself to see Mitch again. After the plane eased to a stop, she unclipped her seat belt and stuffed the gun into her bag.

Mitch left the cockpit and faced her once more. "Please. Don't go alone. Let me help."

Noah unlatched the door and extended the stairs. A blast of arctic air blew into the plane, no more chilled than her heart. "I'm fine," she said. "I know what to do."

Emily went down the stairs and walked toward the small, private-airport terminal. Noah put a hand on Mitch's shoulder, and he glanced up at his older brother.

"She's something else," Noah said quietly.

"Yeah. I screwed up big time. She doesn't trust that I really would do just about anything for her."

"Well, I helped you out." Noah handed him a small unit with a map on the computer screen. A dot slowly moved away from them.

"What is it?"

"I fixed Emily's phone for her. No GPS for the bad guys. No trapping her phone number. But you, little brother, can track her with this. Just don't lose it."

Mitch gave his brother a stunned stare. "You're a hell of a sneak, if I haven't told you that before."

"You let my other interests get out, little brother, and I'll change the code so you can't borrow my Harley."

Mitch sputtered.

"Yeah. I know about the Harley. But you found more than I'll *ever* have, bro. You found someone real in a world of cheats and liars."

"If she'll only give me a chance to prove I'm not one."

Noah slapped him on the back. "If she didn't care, you wouldn't have hurt her so much. Take heart in that. Heck, if you find her son, she'll have to take you back."

Noah took off, and Mitch let his brother's words stew in his mind. He didn't want Emily that way. Not out of some mistaken form of gratitude. He longed for her to want him in the same way he did her. Because he admired her, cared for her…loved her.

Oh, God. He'd fallen in love with her.

The recognition nearly made him sink to his knees. He'd blown it. He'd finally found someone whose loyalty and courage he could respect, whose passion lit a fire within him so hot it consumed his thoughts. And he'd driven her away.

He straightened his shoulders. His feelings didn't matter. All he could focus on was Emily. He made his way to the truck, keeping close watch on her location. The dot had sped up significantly. He turned on his phone, then played through six messages. All but one was from Tanner, ordering him back to the office, threatening him with a suspension and finally to fire him. The last one came from Ian with the news about Marie.

Emily's dot moved farther away. Where was she planning to go? He couldn't think of anywhere safe except Noah's home, and she wouldn't go there. The dot moved toward downtown, back to the first attempt on her life. Why should he be surprised? With Ghost still at large, she was much too vulnerable. He dialed a number.

"Teen Mother's Shelter."

"Sister Kate. It's Mitch Bradford."

"Officer. I was hoping to hear back from you. How are you and Emily doing?"

Mitch winced at the smile in the nun's voice. "Um…that's why I'm calling. Emily's in trouble, Sister. I think she might be heading your way."

"What kind of trouble?"

"Someone wants her dead."

"Ghost?"

"It's more involved than that. Can you hide her? Get her to stay put? I have something to take care of, but I'll be there soon."

"We can hide her, Officer. I'll tell her you're coming—"

"No. Don't do that. She…let's just say we've had a falling-out."

"But you'll be here?"

"She needs protection. It's my job."

Sister Kate laughed. "Oh, boy-o, it's way more than a job. I can hear the feelings in your voice. Don't you fret."

"I won't stop worrying until she's safe," Mitch said, leaving off the one phrase he wanted so badly to say aloud…*in my arms*. "Thank you, Sister."

He hung up the phone. He needed help, and there was only one man he could ask. He just wondered if he'd make it out of his dad's house in one piece.

MITCH PULLED INTO HIS father's driveway. The place hadn't changed much, except for the ramp leading to the front door. Before Mitch even rang the bell, the ex-sergeant opened the door.

"Cameras?" Mitch asked, scanning the perimeter and spying the small electronics in several strategic locations.

"Of course." He reversed his wheelchair to let Mitch enter. "I hadn't expected to see you here."

"Noah didn't call and spill my latest screwup?"

His dad shrugged. "He mentioned you might be by for some intel."

Mitch walked into the living room. The photo of his father and mother still held a place of honor on the fireplace mantel. Short of a few adjustments in the furniture to widen spaces, his dad's place hadn't changed much in the ten years since his mother's death from cancer.

"I need some advice. I'm out of my league, Dad."

"You're a good cop."

"I'm a good SWAT entry man. Emily needs protection, and clearly I can't do it. If I'd been one hundred percent, I would've caught the perp who blew Perry Young's head off. This would be over." He rubbed his leg and took a deep breath. "The problem is, I'm not a detective. And this case is complicated. She needs an investigator. She needs you, not me."

"How's the injury, Mitch?" His father nodded toward the leg. "Really?"

"Fine." Mitch quirked a smile. "Emily hates it when I use that word."

"Means you don't want to talk about it. I get that, son."

"I'm at seventy-five percent. Not good enough for SWAT, and if I can't be SWAT, what's the point?"

His dad pointed to the wheelchair "You're here asking for my help, despite this chair. What makes you think a slightly bum leg makes you less of a cop?"

"You were vice. You used your smarts. That was never me."

"You think on your feet. You strategize quickly. You're good at your job, Mitch. Investigation might be slower paced, but you have a gift for reading people. Better than your brothers or sister. Use your talents. What does your intuition say about the situation?"

"That Emily's going to die if I don't figure this out."

Mitch sank into the couch. He'd never said the words aloud, and he ached with the knowledge that if he couldn't figure out who wanted her gone, he could very well lose Emily, the only woman he'd ever loved. He had to push those emotions aside. He had to focus on the pieces that didn't fit.

"Follow your gut. About the investigation and the girl."

"It feels like there's more than one element, and I'm not seeing the connection. Perry knew a lot, but he's dead. His notes are like a few pieces of a five-thousand-word jigsaw puzzle. I know there's a mole in the Denver PD, but I don't know who."

"You asked me before about Tanner. Is he the mole?"

Mitch shook his head. "I trust him."

"Good enough for me." His dad rolled his wheelchair into an elaborate office. "Ever since you called, I've been doing a bit of *research*. Tanner's financials look good, but I've got the names of four cops who have some interesting data. Two were on duty the night Ghost escaped: Vance and Lincoln. I'm following up."

"Thanks, Dad. Call me if either one hits."

"You got it. And Mitch." His dad rolled over and slapped the back of Mitch's head. "Did you forget everything I ever taught you about women? If you care about them, what's the one thing you never, ever do?"

His father's ability to lecture hadn't changed at all.

"Lie to them. Yeah. Got that." He rounded on his father. "What was I supposed to do? If I'd told her the truth, she would've pushed me out of her life. No one believed her. She needed me. She still needs someone." He paused. "She still needs *me.*"

"You took her to bed."

The accusation hit home. Mitch rubbed the bridge of his nose. "Yeah. I couldn't resist her."

"Not your smartest move, son." His dad looked up at the photo of his mother. "But I understand. Some women melt your brain when they smile."

"You think I got a prayer of salvaging this thing? I care about her. A lot."

"Groveling works well."

"I tried that. She blew me off with the force of an F5 tornado."

"Then prove she can trust you. That's what she wants, son. It's a precious gift."

"That I already threw away."

"Then convince her you've smartened up. That she's too precious to lose."

On the way out to his truck, Mitch took a long look back. Four years ago he'd never have thought to go to his dad for assistance on a case. Strangely, his father's injury had made him a stronger detective.

Mitch didn't dwell on the implications. He slid into the pickup just as an SUV pulled into the driveway.

His brother Chase and sister, Sierra, jumped out, their faces tense and furious.

Mitch met them on the lawn. "Did Noah call you?"

"Our brother is an idiot," Chase said, darkly.

"And you just learned this?" Mitch said.

Sierra shook her head. "I should've known something was up when his techy gadgets started getting cooler than mine. Is he okay? Really?"

"He's fine. We're the ones who need an adjustment." Mitch said. "Go talk to him. You may learn more than you bargain for. I've gotta run."

Sierra placed a hand on his arm. "You're not hurt again, are you?"

He kissed her cheek. "Not in the way you're thinking, little sister."

His brother gave him a speculative glance, but Mitch shook his head. They could talk later. Maybe. Chase had his own demons to battle.

As his brother and sister strode up the sidewalk, Mitch got back into the truck and stared at the tracking device. Emily had made it to Sister Kate's and she wasn't moving. He gunned the accelerator and headed toward the police station. This next hour wouldn't be pretty.

THE DENVER POLICE DEPARTMENT—a place Mitch had called home for a lot of years—didn't feel welcoming right now. He stood and faced his boss. Tanner's face had gone red.

"You might want to calm down, boss. You're going to pop a vein."

"What were you thinking?"

"That we have a mole in this office, and I didn't know who to trust. I couldn't risk Emily's life or losing her son's trail. Not for anyone or anything."

"I thought we had an understanding." Tanner paced up and down his office. "You made me believe you trusted me, Mitch. And you go off and put yourself and Emily at risk. On a hunch after I told you not to leave town, much less the state of Colorado. You should *know* better."

"We might've found her son. I couldn't risk the opportunity slipping away."

His boss thrust his fingers through his short, cropped hair. "Serves me right for giving such an important case to a damn short-timer."

"What do you mean by that?"

"I mean we all know you're going to quit when you can't make the physical for SWAT. I've seen your file, Bradford. You can't cut it. But nobody's brave enough to tell you to your face."

"You don't know that. With Emily's help, my leg's improving. I could make it back." Even to Mitch's ears the words sounded hollow.

"You sure that's the kind of help you're getting? She's your assignment, not your toy."

Mitch grabbed Tanner by the collar. "Shut up."

The detective gripped Mitch's wrists. "Back off. Or I will take you down. No matter how sympathetic I am to your reasons. I want you on desk duty until I decide if I have a use for you. Got it?"

"I'm not leaving Emily stranded. Perry Young may have been a drunk and a gambler, but he was right. This thing is big, and it's ugly."

"Fine," Dane said. "I'll put someone else on it. But you're benched. Starting now."

He'd expected the action and didn't know whether to feel anger or relief. "Then I'm taking sick leave." He spun around and opened the door.

"You don't have any left," his boss called after him.

"Then it's leave without pay. Either way, I'm off duty."

Chapter Twelve

Alone, Emily stretched out on the twin bed in the small room in Sister Kate's shelter, her bag at her side. She pulled out the photo of Joshua and traced the image with her finger. She'd been so close—in her own imagination. Never in reality. "Have I lost you?"

A soft knock sounded on her door. Emily's hand found the cold steel of the weapon in her bag. "Come in."

Heather peeked around the door. "I heard you were back."

Emily motioned the girl in and studied her face. "The bruises have faded a bit."

Heather touched her cheekbones. "I decided not to go back to him."

"I'm glad," Emily said, tucking Joshua's photo under her pillow. "You deserve better. We all deserve someone in our life who puts us before themselves."

"I'm finally starting to believe that," Heather said, tugging at her maternity top. "Sister Kate introduced me to the agency you told me about. They said they can find a good home for my baby."

"What do you think?"

"That I don't have a job, and my family can't help me. That I can't take care of my baby." Tears slid down Heather's cheeks. "I think I have to give her up. Does that make me a bad person?"

Emily stood and wrapped her arms around the girl. "I think it makes you a mother who loves her child more than herself. It makes you a hero."

"I want my baby to be with a family who will love her, but I need to be sure." Heather wiped her eyes. "Snake is going to be really mad."

"Snake?" Emily covered her mouth. "Your boyfriend is really named Snake?"

"Y-yes." Laughter filtered through the room. "Some guy was willing to pay twenty-five thousand dollars if our baby was born with blond hair. Can you believe that? Snake made a deal with the guy. Snake would do anything for that kind of money." Heather caressed her abdomen. "Even sell his daughter."

Emily's hand stilled on Heather's back. She met the girl's teary gaze. "I need to talk to your boyfriend. Would you be willing to call Snake for me? Lie to him?"

Heather paused, uncertain. "Would I have to see him?"

"No, but I need to know who's involved in taking these babies, Heather. Your boyfriend could be the key to finding my little boy."

"You've been so nice to me, Mrs. W. I'll call him."

"Get your phone while I write down what I want you to say."

Emily's pulse pounded, a flicker of hope reigniting. She could create an imaginary Scandinavian husband who wanted a blond-haired girl who looked like him. The adoption agency might very well contact Snake. It was worth a shot. Emily looked down at her clothes. No way would this sell her as a wealthy want-to-be mother. She'd have to go back to the house. Find something appropriate.

Within a half hour Emily had absconded with Sister Kate's keys. The nun had argued with her, but Emily had assured her she'd be right back. She struggled to find the gear on the ancient Impala and headed toward home.

As she reached the curve, she sucked in a deep breath. Eric's cross was still bare. "What did you know, Eric? What didn't you tell me?"

The memorial had no answers, and neither did she. Emily pulled down the street and studied the house she and Eric had bought together. Yellow crime-scene tape blocked the door, but that wouldn't stop her. Her key slipped easily into the lock, and she pushed into her home.

"I knew you'd come back eventually."

Emily froze. Ghost rose from the sofa. A line of opened wine bottles, crackers, cheese and trash littered the coffee table.

She clutched her bag closer, taking comfort in the heavy metal inside. "You've made yourself at home," she said, her words coming out slowly, feeling her way for the weapon. Just a few more seconds.

"Unfinished business," he said with an arrogant grin.

"We certainly have that." Emily pulled out the Glock and held it on the man who had come to symbolize her search for her son.

Ghost paused and then smiled, his glittering teeth giving her a glimpse of how he must've charmed all those young girls to give their babies away.

"Who's your contact?" she asked. "Where do you take those girls?"

"I have a lot of contacts, Mrs. Wentworth. A certain police officer you know very well, for example."

She shook her head. "Mitch would never—"

"Interesting." He continued to grin. "You assumed I meant your lover. I could've meant his boss, or a beat cop who roams around the neighborhood. You can never tell the good guys from the bad guys these days."

"I know which one you are," Emily said, disgust lacing her tone. "You take advantage of those teenagers."

"They're sluts. They get what they want. Money and no kid to take care of. I'm providing a valuable service." Ghost grabbed one of the wine bottles that Eric had taken so much pride in collecting and tipped it back. "You want your son?"

Emily nodded her head, her hand still steady on the weapon.

"You'd do anything, wouldn't you?" Ghost muttered with a smirk.

"Yes." She swallowed back the eagerness and tried to remain calm. She could do this. For Joshua's sake.

"Then come with me. Come with me, and I'll show you where your son is."

He could be lying, but she'd believed from the beginning that Ghost could lead her to Joshua.

"I keep my weapon."

Ghost took another step forward. "I don't think so." He smiled and kicked the coffee table aside. "You don't have the guts to shoot me."

With a howl, he launched his body at her, arms outstretched.

Emily squeezed the trigger.

MITCH STARED IN DISBELIEF at the tracking map. Sister Kate had promised to keep an eye on her. Why had Emily gone back to her house? He gunned the accelerator forward just as the radio he'd pilfered from the police department squawked to life.

"Report of shots fired…"

When the dispatcher quoted Emily's address, Mitch cursed and floored the gas pedal. She could be injured. Or worse. If anything happened to Emily…

He couldn't bear the thought. It would be his fault. He

should've locked her up to keep her safe even if she hated him for it. At least he'd know she was okay.

Sirens wailed behind him as he flew up the mountainside, but he didn't care. Let them arrest him…once he knew Emily was okay.

He focused on navigating the sharp turns, nearly running into an old, junky Impala trundling down the hill, until a loud beeping sounded at his side. He glanced at the tracking system. Emily was on the move again. And she'd just passed him.

His gaze hit his rearview mirror. He could barely make out the taillights of the Impala rounding a curve when his phone rang. Mitch punched the speakerphone as he searched for a place to make a U-turn on the mountain road.

"What the hell are you doing?" Tanner barked. "I've got officers in pursuit of Noah's car, with you at the wheel, I presume, and shots at Emily Wentworth's home address. You are so fired."

"Fine. Fire me. Emily was at the house. Now she's headed back down the mountain. Or at least her phone is."

"How do you know?"

"The cell has a tracking device planted in it," Mitch muttered.

"You keep after the signal. If Emily's in the car, we want to know. We'll check out the house. I'll get back to you. But, Bradford, we are having a *long* conversation before you're back in my unit."

"Dane." Mitch had to trust his instincts again. "Work with Lieutenant Decker to pick your team. I trust him. No one else."

"Will do, Mitch. I'll keep in touch."

Mitch dropped his phone on the seat. For ten minutes he tracked the Impala but couldn't quite catch up. Whoever drove it knew downtown Denver like the back of their hand.

Finally, the phone rang.

"Bradford."

"Emily's not here," Tanner said quietly.

The hesitation in the man's voice made Mitch's gut churn. "But…"

"The house is pretty trashed. There's blood spatter in the living room. Someone's hurt."

Mitch gripped the steering wheel and glanced at his side. "According to my tracker, the car's stopped."

"Where are you? I've got the lieutenant and his team on standby."

"Coming up on Fifth and Colfax." He caught sight of the car, and two figures disappearing into an abandoned apartment building, one slight, with a sway of hips he recognized all too well. Thank God. His heart started beating again for the first time since he'd heard the notification of shots. "I see her. With a big guy in a trench coat. Might be Ghost. They went into that old apartment building on Sixth."

"I know it. I'll get the team there. Wait for us, Mitch."

"As long as I can."

He stabbed the off button. Without any intel, he had no idea what he was walking into. All he knew was Emily was trapped inside.

He flipped his collar up and walked down the street, passing the Impala. Streaks of red smeared the front seat.

Blood.

GHOST SHOVED THE GUN into Emily's side and she staggered through the door of the decrepit apartment building. All but one of the windows were boarded shut. The place looked abandoned.

"Get me upstairs to the first room on the left," he rasped. "Don't talk to anyone or you and them are dead." They trudged up, and Emily studied the layout and each young girl's face she met as they climbed the stairs and entered the room.

A square-jawed man with a military haircut stomped into the room behind them. "What the hell happened to you? And what's *she* doing here? Are you crazy?"

"Sit down and shut up, Vance," Ghost said as he flopped back on the bed.

He pulled away the bloody hand from his side. "Witch shot me, but I got her here. Get me some disinfectant and some bandages, will you?"

"You need the doc?"

"Nah. She grazed my side. Some butterflies'll hold me for now." Ghost propped himself up against the back of the bed, still aiming the Glock he'd wrestled away from Emily. "Once we find out what she knows, we'll take care of her. I have to waste that kid, Ricky, too. He's still poking around." He glared at Vance. "You should've taken him out—"

"Shut up," Vance said.

As he handed Ghost the medical supplies, Emily caught sight of a badge hanging out of his pocket. He was the cop.

"I had a bigger target. That warning shot should've shut her up." He glared at Emily. "Doesn't matter now. Once our problem upstairs is taken care of, Ricky won't make trouble anymore. If he does, he and his grandmother will let a cop into the house. No one will care if an old lady and kid bite the dust. I'll plant drugs or something."

His calculated plan made Emily shiver. She'd thought maybe she could reason with one of them. This cop had gone all the way bad.

"We'll make it two for one, today," Vance added. "Keep our exposure to a minimum."

"Not a bad idea. How long 'til she pops?"

"A few hours. Maybe less. Boss doesn't want it done here, though. The last one pushed Marie over the edge. The idiot stole my data on my *guest*—" he nodded toward Emily "—and went to that drunk PI. Nearly blew everything. Doc doesn't want any more screwups. We kill them off site."

The man said the words as if taking someone's life was business as usual. A strange calmness came over Emily. She had the next few hours to find a way out. And, if nothing else, to come up with a way to get a message to Mitch. Despite everything, Emily recognized he would keep searching for Joshua, even if she were gone. She needed more information.

"You told me you'd tell me where my son is," she blurted.

"I lied," Ghost said. "We didn't take your damn kid, but you ask too many questions. You should've left it alone. Snake and Heather's baby was worth half a million bucks. Both blond-haired and blue-eyed. That's why we paid him to get her pregnant. Then you had to go and ruin the deal."

Emily's head spun. They didn't know where Joshua was. She didn't understand. "But Perry—"

"Young?" Vance laughed. "That fool stumbled onto the operation. That's why I had to take him out. He knew too much."

This couldn't be happening. She had to get away. To find Joshua and to warn Heather. Emily squirmed in her chair and wrapped her coat tighter around her, then shoved her hands in the pockets. Her fingers hit the metal of her cell phone. She clutched it, and her gaze flew to the men. If they would just leave her alone, she could call Mitch or 911. He'd find her. He'd save her.

She could count on him.

The truth filled Emily's heart with awe. She could count on Mitch Bradford. He'd lied, but he wouldn't let her down. She moved her fingers over the on button.

"Hey, there. What're you doing?" Vance grabbed Emily and yanked her to her feet. "You search her?" he asked Ghost.

"She shot me. I got the gun. Exactly when—"

"Idiot." Vance tugged her coat off and patted her down.

Emily shivered as his hands lingered over her breasts. He squeezed them and then pushed her down in the chair. Maybe he wouldn't look in the pocket.

He grabbed the coat and snagged the cell phone. "Fool." Vance pressed a couple of buttons. "No calls for the past half hour. You dodged a bullet, dude. The doc would've had me kill you, too, if she'd led the cops here."

Vance dropped her phone on the floor and rammed the heel of his boot into it, smashing the small device, then tossed it into a sink and ran water over it. "No cavalry."

His satisfied smile squeezed out most of Emily's hope. She'd put herself in this position, and now Joshua would never know that his mother had loved him very much.

Ghost finished applying several butterfly strips and pulled down his bloody sweater. "That'll do me. I'm changing, and then I gotta dump the car. Take care of her."

He pushed up his sleeves, and Emily saw the red-and-green devil tattoo. Her head ached, her mind whirled. It wasn't right. Something was missing.

Oh, God. Ghost wasn't the man from that night. Perry had been right.

"She'll be fine in here," Vance said. "One less room to wipe down for trace evidence."

They closed her in, and the sound of the door bolting sealed Emily's fate. Once the poor girl's baby was born, both of them were dead. Mitch didn't know about Ghost or Vance. Unless Emily found a way out.

MITCH HAD SEARCHED THE entire perimeter of the building and didn't see an opening. Odd. Usually an abandoned building like this wasn't so heavily fortified. All the windows appeared boarded. He needed intel. No way to know how many people were inside. Emily had disappeared five minutes ago. It felt like a lifetime.

How the hell was he supposed to get in? He had to be smart, or Emily was dead.

A familiar black van pulled down an alley nearby. Yes.

Lieutenant Decker jumped out, and his SWAT teammates followed. Mitch edged in the alleyway, out of the line of sight of the apartment building.

"Give us the sit rep," Lieutenant Decker ordered as the team surrounded Mitch.

Mitch spoke quickly and succinctly.

Decker nodded toward one of the other entry men, Reynolds. "Find us a way in."

"You got it, Lieutenant."

"Roof?" Mason, the sniper, asked, indicating a building across the street.

"That's your best bet," Decker said. "Keep a lookout for any activity."

"Our hostage. Can she help us?" Reynolds asked.

"She thinks she's alone in this," Mitch said. "With good reason. She doesn't trust the police department."

"Great," Decker muttered. "Does she trust you?"

"To save her life. Maybe. Otherwise, no."

Lieutenant Decker lifted his brow. "Man, Mitch. What trouble have you gotten yourself into? I heard Tanner was trying to palm you off to summons duty this morning."

"Long story."

"In position, Alpha Leader," Mason's voice came across the radio.

"Ten-four."

"What's the risk if we ram?" Greggson, the number-two entry man, sidled up to Decker and Mitch.

"Ghost, the guy I believe took her, lures pregnant girls off the streets. Then they disappear. I know of one girl, Kayla

Foster, who's missing. Another teenager ended up dead postpartum."

Greggson let out a violent curse. "A real winner."

"We could have a bunch of pregnant teens in that building," Mitch warned. "You gotta go in careful."

"Any way we can talk our way in?"

"Alpha One to Alpha Leader." Mason's voice crackled over the radio. "I've got movement. Second floor. Southeast corner. Someone just shifted a board."

Mitch grabbed the lieutenant's binoculars and peered at the window. Cobalt blue eyes stared out the small gap. He'd recognize them anywhere.

"Emily," he breathed. "She's amazing." Her fingers slipped around the second slab. "She's using metal to pry the wood away from the window."

Decker ripped back his binoculars. "Assuming she's locked in—and I doubt she'd try to break out of a second-story window if she weren't—putting someone in her room might give us an advantage."

"I can slip in and get her out," Mitch said.

"How's your leg?"

"Good enough for this."

Decker studied him. "All right." The lieutenant handed him an earpiece and a black tool bag. "Get in position. Reynolds and Greggson will pull you up."

Within minutes, Mitch had the harness around him and was walking up the side of the building. No alarm had sounded. Those inside had figured a few condemned signs would keep people away. That and a paid-off cop.

When he reached the window, he made a quick cutting motion with his hand. He dangled thirty feet above the ground. Emily's fingertips were clutched around the second board.

"Emily?"

The top of her head peered out, and her eyes widened when she saw him. Then they softened in relief. "I knew you'd come."

Then she smiled. Mitch's heart thudded against his chest.

"Stand back," he said. She nodded and moved away from the window. He quickly pried the boards from their hinges before sliding through the window.

Emily launched herself at him the second he touched down. He wrapped his arms around her and held her close. "Are you okay? You're not hurt?"

She shook her head, burying deeper against him, hugging him tight as if she would never let him go.

"There was blood at your house," he said, unable to keep the harshness from his voice.

"Ghost. I shot him."

He set her back from him and unfastened the harness. He couldn't stop grinning at her. "You are one spectacular woman."

He hugged her close again, relishing the feel of her small body against his, her breasts pressed hard against him. "They're going to kill me," she whispered. "And another girl. She's having a baby, and after she delivers they plan to get rid of both of us. We have to help her."

He took one last breath, inhaled the scent of her, one last second to hug her close, then stepped away. "How many girls? How many guarding them?"

"I don't know. I heard some teenagers laughing up and down the hall, so I don't think everyone's being held against their will. There's a police officer. Vance. He killed Perry. He's the one who shot at us, too. Just a warning," Emily said bitterly. "A doctor is here, too. And Ghost, but he said he was going to move Sister Kate's car. That's everyone I saw."

"You practically took a tour." Mitch smiled. "Good job." His dad had also been right about Vance. Mitch relayed the information to Lieutenant Decker. If Ghost exited the building, he could provide SWAT's access opportunity.

Mitch bent to Emily and kissed her. "We're going to get everyone out of here. I promise." Mitch knelt in front of the door, testing the lock. "I wanted to send you out the window, but the SWAT team is moving into position. No time."

"I heard the dead bolt shut."

"Not a problem," Mitch said as he pulled out a small tension wrench and eased it into the bottom of the lock and stabbed a pick above it. Two tries and the lock gave way. He pulled the pick out and slowly turned the wrench. "Voila."

"You learned that in SWAT?"

"Nah. Noah taught me how to sneak back into the house when I was about fourteen."

He communicated the new status to Lieutenant Decker.

"We'll stay put for a few minutes. The guys are set up outside to see if Ghost exits. That way they can go in quiet."

Emily studied Mitch's face. He looked energized and alive.

"This is the life you want. The excitement," she said quietly.

He turned his head. "I'm good at it. And yeah, I like catching the bad guys."

"You'll get back, Mitch. Your leg will improve enough to do the job. Then you can have what you want."

He laced his fingers through hers. "What if I want you, too?"

Before she could reply, a clanging alarm sounded in the hallway.

"Okay, girls, back into your rooms. Looks like we've got a new arrival almost here."

The jolly voice made Emily shudder in revulsion.

"The doctor," she said. "The baby's coming."

"We're out of time, but he's also made it easier. If everyone's in their rooms, we can make this thing happen safely."

Mitch tapped his earpiece.

With a quick relay of more intel, Mitch turned to Emily. "They have Ghost. They're coming in. Doing a room-to-room. You stay here. They'll come get you."

"Where are you going?"

"To find the room with the doctor."

He shoved a weapon into her hand. "Don't shoot the SWAT team. Officer Vance, on the other hand, feel free to take aim. There's nothing I hate more than a traitor."

He slipped out of the door, his stealth movements dangerous.

She gripped the gun in her hand and stood near the door, expecting screams or shuffling, but it was utterly silent.

A few minutes later, her hand had cramped around the gun. The lock turned. "It's SWAT, Mrs. Wentworth," a voice said softly.

An arm covered in black eased through a crack in the door. A split second later, a man had pivoted and stripped her of her weapon. "I'm Reynolds. Good to meet you. Now come with me."

Emily stepped out of the room, covered by the large SWAT team member. About four pregnant teens were being rushed down the stairs, a couple being carried with hands over their mouths.

Vance rounded the corner in a dead run. He headed toward Emily. Mitch plowed after him.

"Vance. Stop!"

Reynolds pushed her down, covering her body before taking aim at the errant cop.

"Bitch," Vance screamed and leaped at her.

Chapter Thirteen

Mitch caught Vance from the side and shoved him away from Emily. The man slammed into the floor, and with a quick move, Mitch pinned Vance to the ground and forced his hands behind his back. Mitch had to stop himself from taking a cheap shot at the guy who'd gone after her. "You're going down."

Reynolds stood and helped Emily to her feet. "Nice move. You back?"

"Almost." Although the ache in Mitch's leg indicated a SWAT assignment wouldn't happen anytime soon.

Reynolds knelt down and fastened zip ties around Vance's wrists. "Where's the doctor, traitor?"

"I wasn't doing anything wrong." Vance glared at them. "I just followed you guys in."

Emily stalked over to the man on the floor. Mitch could see the fury vibrating from within her.

"You were going to kill me," she said.

"Liar," Vance spat.

Mitch tugged the man to his feet and spun him around against the wall. He closed his fingers around the soon-to-be-ex-cop's neck.

Emily rushed behind Mitch, leaning over his back. The woman was fearless.

"You know something about my son. I know you do." Her husky voice had gone desperate.

"Idiot. Your son was never here. You were chasing the wrong devil from the beginning." Vance laughed.

Emily sagged against Mitch. "No. *Someone* here knows *something*. They just have to."

He shoved his arm harder against the guy's throat. "Unless you want me telling every inmate you're a cop, you give up the doctor's location. I find out you're lying, you won't last a week inside."

Vance went ghost-white and deflated like the coward he was. "Fourth floor. Insulated room so the other girls don't flip out when they hear them scream."

"What's the layout?" Mitch snapped. "And how do I get in without tipping him off?"

Their prisoner spilled the description of the room. "Doc's waiting for the midwife. She's not here yet, but he'll expect a knock on the door."

Mitch passed off Vance to another of his teammates, then turned to Emily. "Go with them. I want you outside."

She shook her head. "I can help. If he's really expecting a woman, I can get him to open the door for me. Otherwise, you place the girl in the room at risk if he panics."

"She's right," Reynolds said quietly.

Mitch wanted nothing more than to get Emily away from this place, but they were running out of time. "Get Vance out of here," he told Reynolds. "Emily, stay behind me," he ordered.

They ran up the stairs to the fourth floor, meeting Greggson at the top.

"All clear, except at the end," he said. "But check this out."

They followed him into a space with a wall full of monitors showing every room in the house.

Mitch cursed. "They knew we were here?"

"I don't think so," Greggson said. "This area was deserted when we arrived."

Mitch looked at the sea of empty rooms. Except one. Kayla lay on a bed, her legs bound in stirrups, but she was fighting against the bonds. "That's Kayla Foster. Does this thing have volume?"

Greggson flicked a few switches and turned a knob. The man in the white coat smiled, his face cold and terrifying. "Finally dilated enough, my little troublemaker. It won't be long now. After we deliver your brat, we're getting rid of you. Just like your friend."

"What did you do to Vanessa?" Her forehead damp with sweat and her face streaked with tears, Kayla cried out as another contraction began.

"She's not your concern anymore. Just push the brat out, or I'll cut it out," he said, nodding to the tray of instruments at his side.

"No. Don't hurt my baby." Kayla's plea echoed through the speaker.

"That's it. No more time. We're getting her out of there now." Mitch updated Decker and turned to Emily. "The room is soundproofed, so I'll knock loudly. You announce yourself, then move aside. That'll get the doctor away from her. Greggson, you go for the doctor. I'll get the girl."

They moved into position, and Mitch knocked on the door. He nodded at Emily.

"Doctor. I'm here," she shouted and flattened herself against the opposite wall.

The door slid open. "It's about time."

"Go!" Greggson's voice sounded in Mitch's ear.

They rushed through the door side by side. Mitch reached Kayla just as Greggson slammed the doctor against the wall and restrained his wrists.

Once Greggson had the doctor secure with zip ties, Emily

raced into the room and covered Kayla with a sheet, then knelt beside her, whispering words of comfort, holding her as the teen sobbed in her arms.

"How's she doing?" Mitch asked, his concern for the girl growing as she cried out in pain.

"Her contractions are coming fast. She needs a hospital."

Mitch barked out an order. Greggson communicated with Lieutenant Decker. Minutes later, paramedics were loading Kayla onto a gurney. She clutched Mitch's arm. "Coach? Can you call my grandma? I need her."

Mitch pushed back the blond hair from Kayla's damp forehead. "You got it, honey. I'll let Ricky know, too."

She shook her head against the pillow on the gurney. "I let him down."

"He loves you. He had faith in you. He knew something was wrong. That's why he searched for you."

A tear slipped down her cheek. "The doctor took Vanessa, and I haven't seen her since. Have you found her?"

Mitch met Emily's sorrowful gaze. "Let's get you to the hospital, Kayla. Then we can fill you in."

Kayla wiped the tears away. "Don't bother. He killed her, didn't he?" She looked at the doctor, now sitting in the corner of the room being questioned by Greggson. "It's all my fault."

Emily leaned in closer. "No, Kayla. You can't control what other people do."

"You don't understand. Vanessa and I changed our minds about giving up our babies, but we were stupid. We came back to tell the doctor. He was really mad and told us we had no choice." Kayla rubbed her eyes and raised a haunted gaze to them. "I told Vanessa we should pretend to change our minds and wait for an opportunity to sneak out. It was working. Until the night I wanted some milk from the kitchen. We were halfway down the stairs when we saw *him*."

Mitch instincts trilled in his mind. "Who? Vance? The cop?"

"Not him. A man. With a tattoo. He was yelling about needing a signature. He threatened the doctor. Scared him. Bad. Then Vanessa gasped. A contraction. The doctor saw us." Kayla wiped her eyes. "I never saw her again."

Mitch leaned over Kayla. "What kind of tattoo did this guy have?"

"The same gang tat as Ghost—a red and green devil on his wrist—but with a pink ribbon wrapped around it. Like those breast-cancer ribbons. Weird."

"Knife!" Greggson gave a shout as a loud crash reverberated through the room.

Mitch whirled toward the noise, shoving Emily behind him to protect her. The doctor knocked the surgical tray into them as he bolted from the corner and out the door.

"He stabbed me with a syringe." Greggson held the side of his neck. "Careful! He must've palmed a scalpel. He cut the zip ties."

Mitch cursed and bolted down the hall after the doctor, all the while relaying a message to Reynolds. How had a secure scene gone downhill so fast?

The doctor grabbed the banister and tried to rush down the stairs, but by the time he reached the second floor, he was panting and doubled over. Mitch took the stairs two at a time, each jolt slamming up his leg like a firebrand. He'd pay for it later, but right now he didn't care. He'd seen Vanessa's crime-scene photos. Mitch was taking this murderer down.

He was just feet behind the doctor when the man frantically looked around and veered into the same bedroom Mitch and Emily escaped from earlier. Mitch followed. The missing window slats allowed the sun to bathe the room in light.

"Don't come any closer." The doctor paced frantically, brandishing the scalpel and searching for an escape.

"Mitch, find out what was in that syringe," Reynolds said through the earpiece. "Fast."

Mitch closed him and the doctor into the room. Alone. "There's nowhere to go, and I'm not feeling friendly. So, Doc, what was in that syringe?"

"Nothing but air," the doctor snapped. "If done right, it's the perfect crime."

"You catch that?" Mitch said through his earpiece.

"Air embolus," the EMT said sharply. "Get Greggson to the hospital."

"He'll be fine," the doctor said bitterly. "It was a little bubble. I didn't even have time to hit a vein."

"Lucky for you."

"Oh, yeah, I really feel lucky now. Everything I've worked for is gone. Because of that nosy do-gooder."

Emily slammed into the room. "Who was the man with the tattoo? The one with the pink ribbon on it? The one you're afraid of?"

The doctor's eyes went wide; his face paled to a grayish-white. "No way I'm talking. They'll kill me."

"I knew it." Emily rushed forward. "Who are *they*?"

"Emily! Don't—"

The doctor grabbed her before Mitch could move.

"Stay back or I'll kill her. I got nothing left to lose." He held the scalpel to her throat and backed toward the window.

Mitch knew the man was telling the truth. He'd kill Emily. Mitch forced his pounding pulse to slow. He had to be smart. "Doc, we can work something out."

The guy wasn't listening. He clutched her tighter, shaking his head. "I shouldn't have let Ghost talk me into helping the guy. Easy money, Ghost said," the doctor muttered. "Just a birth certificate that looked legal. I didn't know who he really was. How could I know?"

"Please. Tell me," Emily begged. "Who has my son?"

Her eyes had taken on the desperate look Mitch had seen before. She struggled against the doctor, and he cursed. The blade nicked her neck, drawing blood. She gasped. Her eyes turned glassy. Mitch recognized the signs. Flashback. She pulled and jerked within her captor's arms, unseeing, screaming.

"Get away from me. No! I can't see your face. Don't kill me. Don't take my baby!" Tears streamed down Emily's face. Her agonized cries broke Mitch's heart.

"Are you crazy?" the doctor yelled. "Don't move or I'll slit your throat open." Suddenly Emily stilled, almost deadly serene. He took another step back, dragging her with him. Mitch couldn't tell if she was in shock or had come out of it. The situation could explode any second.

"I want immunity and witness protection."

"Doc, just let her go and we'll discuss it." Mitch lowered his voice to a calm, easy tone.

"I don't have time to talk. I can't let you take me in. I won't last a day in jail. They'll get to me. They can get to anyone."

"I believe you. But you have to show good faith. I need to let my bosses know you're a reasonable man. And that you're telling the truth. Give me something. A name. Proof."

"You're not listening." The doctor backed closer to the window, Emily plastered against him as a shield. "I'll jump. I'll take her with me."

"No!" Suddenly, Emily wrenched away, but to Mitch's horror, the doctor held on. Instead of falling into the center of the room, she stumbled closer to the window. The doctor shoved her hard at the opening.

Mitch dove toward her, slamming down on his bad knee but knocking her out of the way. The doctor tripped over their falling bodies, and his momentum carried him over the edge. Mitch twisted and grabbed the man's coat, ignoring the searing pains shooting through his leg with blinding intensity. He couldn't pass out. Hell, a full breath would be nice.

Emily gripped the material to help Mitch hang on to the doctor as he dangled from the window.

"Save me," he screamed. "Don't let me fall."

Mitch struggled to adjust his hold on the coat and, grimacing, got on his knees. "Give me a name," he said, reaching one hand down.

"Frankie," the doctor panted. "Please, help me up."

Mitch braced himself, and he and Emily tugged the man up by the coat until their hands almost touched the doctor's. Suddenly, with a loud tearing sound, the white garment gave way. The fabric split. Frantically, Mitch clutched for the man's hand, or another part of the coat, but it was no use. The doctor fell to the ground, screaming, until his head slammed against the hard cement below and there was silence.

Mitch leaned through the open window and stared at white, sightless eyes staring back at him.

Emily hugged Mitch from behind. "We did everything we could," she said softly.

"It wasn't enough." He turned into her arms and held her closer.

Shouts from below penetrated their momentary quiet.

"Mitch, you guys okay?" Decker called through the microphone.

"Fine. We're coming down," he said.

"Do you think Frankie is the man with the tattoo?" Emily asked.

"I don't know, but we're going to find out." Mitch turned, and his leg collapsed under him, spasms firing up his knee and leg. He clenched his jaw to keep from turning the air a colorful shade of blue, then pulled himself up into a seated position.

She knelt beside him. "What happened?"

He gave her a small smile. "Nothing. Knee popped. Just give me a minute. I'll be fine."

He was lying through his gritted teeth, and Emily could see right through him. He had a feeling that this injury might very well nail the coffin shut for returning to SWAT. Strangely, the prospect didn't devastate him as much as he'd thought it would. The injury was worth it, because Emily was safe.

He hugged her tight. She'd come too close to dying. "Don't worry about me, Emily. I'm okay. There's a lot of cleanup ahead. An adoption agency to bring down and a lot of babies to find, but right now, we need to locate Frankie and hope he's the man with the tattoo."

FRANK MANGINO ANSWERED the summons, his nerves close to breaking. He'd been on edge for a full year, but the past week had been hell. He stepped into his uncle's office, and his stomach clenched when he noticed the man to his uncle's right side. Great, just great.

"Uncle Sal. Mr. Wentworth."

His boss didn't smile in greeting. "I had an interesting call from a friend at the police department, Frank. There's an inquiry about a suspect with a rather unique tattoo on his wrist."

Frank's hand involuntarily covered the colorful devil inked there.

"Let me see it," his uncle snapped. "Now."

Frank walked forward and pushed up his sleeve. The red and green devil identified him with a gang he'd joined when he'd been a stupid kid.

"I told you to have it removed," his uncle said.

"It reminds me," Frank said, "of family."

"And why the pink ribbon?"

Frank looked at his uncle in disbelief. "For Francesca. Or don't you remember her?"

"Your sister's cancer and her inability to have children was a tragedy, but a mark like that identifies you. Especially after the stunt you pulled on Emily Wentworth. Blowing up her vehicle. I recognized the signature the second I saw it on the news."

Frank shifted his eyes away from his uncle. "She wouldn't give up. She was starting to remember the night of the accident."

"Another failure on your part. You were supposed to kill them all. That was our agreement with Mr. Wentworth. Now the cops are looking for that tattoo because you were fool enough to go to that doctor for a birth certificate. You let down the family. I can't allow it to go unpunished."

William Wentworth stalked up to him. "What did you do with my brother's son? The kid's not dead, either, is he?"

Frank backed away, his gaze darting to the exit. Could he make it?

William grabbed Frank by the throat. "Don't try it." William's grip tightened. "I know the answer to my question. I did a little research and found the truth too fast, Frankie. Your sister from Oklahoma adopted a baby boy last year. Amazing when she tried to go through legal channels for so long and failed. She was a bad risk. Cancer took her ability to have children, and her capacity to adopt."

William shoved Frank away and he eased toward the door. Just a few steps more.

"I don't think so, Frankie." His uncle lifted a gun.

Frank stared down the barrel. "Uncle Sal?"

"Sorry, kid. You made one too many mistakes. Loyalty only goes so far."

The gun went off, and a white-hot burn exploded in his

chest. Clutching his shirt, now wet with blood, he slid to the floor, reaching out to try to break his fall.

Sal turned to William. "I'll get the boys to clean this up."

"Fifteen years ago you made a deal with my father when he agreed to launder your money through the company. You were supposed to protect us. You failed."

"I know, but it can be fixed," Sal said. "I'll take care of everything."

"You and Frankie had your chance, you idiot." William Wentworth spat on Frank. "I'll have to stop Emily myself, or we're screwed."

Sal stood up, his gaze narrowed. "Don't go high-and-mighty on me, William. Your brother's the one who started this mess when he called that detective. No loyalty in your family, is there?"

"It was her fault," William muttered. "Goody Two-shoes. Eric turned his back on all of us. For her."

Frank felt blood gurgle up through his lips as William walked over to him. He slipped on gloves, reached down and removed Frank's weapon from his waistband.

"Sorry, Sal. I have loose ends to tie up." William turned and fired.

Sal slumped over his desk, then tried to raise his own gun. But William grabbed it from his hand. "You're both expendable."

The light left Sal's eyes as blood pooled around him.

William placed the gun he'd shot Sal with in Frank's hand and fired another round. Frank groaned.

"Still alive? Good." He took Sal's gun and pointed it at Frank's head. "No one lies to me and gets away with it. But in this case, Frankie, I'll end your life quick since I can use Joshua to salvage this mess. Thanks to you, when Emily Wentworth dies along with her son's kidnappers—Francesca and her husband—I'll become the hero who saved my nephew."

"No!" Frank hadn't meant for anything to happen to his sister.

A flash of smoke from the gun's barrel was the last thing he saw. *I'm sorry, Francesca. So sorry.*

EMILY DIDN'T KNOW HOW long it had taken Mitch to wrap up the scene. As she walked into the police department beside him, her entire body sore, her heart aching with loss, her mind rebelled against her mistake. She'd been certain that the doctor knew where Joshua was. Now she knew it had been a dead end. Except for one name.

"We're close," Mitch said. "I can feel it."

"I was wrong about the adoption ring."

"Not really. The man with the tattoo went there. We have a name. We'll find him."

Emily couldn't get over the determination in Mitch's voice. Her mind whirled. He'd lied to her from the moment they'd met, and yet he still fought for her. Could those actions erase his dishonesty? Was truth more than what Mitch had said? Was truth really in his every action? "You never give up, do you?"

"Not in my nature." Mitch gave her a slight shrug.

"So, how do we find Frankie?" she asked.

"Ghost's tat is a gang tattoo. We search the database for the gang members we've arrested. With any luck, we'll find him."

Mitch gave her a small smile and clasped her hand in his. He brought her palm to his lips. Emily shivered at the warmth of his touch, and her heart calmed. They would find Joshua. Together. There was still hope. Mitch had given that to her.

She stared at his strong jaw, and her heart swelled. She'd only known him a few days, but as she stared at their entwined fingers, she couldn't imagine her life without him next to her. Without one of his jokes, or looking into the mischievous glint in his eyes and wondering what he'd planned next. At times she'd wondered if it was just adrenaline that made her heart race whenever he came near, but it was so much more. She couldn't picture finding Joshua without Mitch at her side, without them as a family afterward. She could see a future with him.

Oh, my God. Emily stopped.

Did she love him?

He looked over at her. "What? Did you remember something?"

She turned and laid her hand on his cheek. "You're an amazing man."

He furrowed his brow. "We haven't found him yet, Emily."

"I know, but—"

"Mitch, Emily." Dane Tanner crossed the floor and greeted them. "I have someone I think you'll want to talk to. She's in the conference room."

Emily sighed. This wasn't the time.

They followed Detective Tanner. Mitch opened the door for Emily, and she stilled. Victoria Wentworth sat at the table, hands folded, trying to look calm, but Emily could see the redness in her eyes and the trembling in her fingertips. This was not a Victoria she knew.

The woman rose from her seat, unsteady, almost swaying, but proud as ever. She flashed a withering glance at Tanner. "I said I'd talk to Officer Bradford. I'm here because of Eric, but *she* has no business in this room. If she stays, I'm leaving."

With that, Victoria turned away. Tanner let out a slow breath.

Emily stared at Victoria's rigid posture. The possibilities she'd nurtured when Eric was alive had been foolish. "It could have been so different between us, Mrs. Wentworth, if you'd let it. We both lost Eric."

"You stole my son from me," Victoria said coldly.

"You shoved him away," Emily whispered. "He always loved you. Wanted you in our lives. Wanted you to come to know Joshua. That will be your loss." Without another glance, Emily pushed out of the conference room.

Mitch followed her, resting his hand on her back. "You okay?"

Emily gave him a regretful smile. "I expected too much. Why is that?"

He kissed her cheek. "Because you believe the best in everyone else, no matter what they do to you. It's one of the things I really admire about you."

Emily stared up at him. She gripped his hands in hers. "Go in there. Victoria's not here for me. If she deigned to come down to the police station, it's for a reason. I'll be waiting."

Mitch leaned into her. "See if you can find a place to hole up for a while." He kissed her forehead, then her eyes and finally gave her a soft, tender kiss on her lips. "You need to rest. With Vance arrested, the station should be safe now. I'll be as quick as I can. Then we'll identify Frankie."

He disappeared behind the conference-room door, leaving Emily alone in the foyer of the police station. She sighed and started toward the waiting area.

"Emily—" Her brother-in-law stepped just inside the building. "Thank God, I found you. I've been looking everywhere."

He seemed excited and flushed, appearing nothing like the calm businessman she was used to seeing.

"William, what's wrong? I know your mother—"

He shook his head. "No, it's Joshua. I think I've found Joshua!"

Emily's knees buckled. Her heart raced. "It can't be," she breathed.

William led her toward the exit. "You were right all along, Emily." He looked down at the floor, his embarrassment obvious. "I should have supported your search no matter what. I never should have listened to Mother and Father. There were things happening in the company that I didn't understand then. Things with my father…"

She grabbed his wool coat. "Where is my son, William? Where's Joshua?"

"We have to handle this carefully. I don't have proof yet. I'm checking into things, but there's a baby I need you to see who I think is Joshua. He looks just like Eric's pictures at the same age. Will you come with me?"

"Of course." She pushed through the door. "But what makes you think this is Joshua?"

William hurried toward his car, his cheeks flushed. "I found out a man who works for me is involved with some shady dealings—adoption rings, murder. I should've known when I saw the gang tattoo—"

"Wait a minute. He had a tattoo? Describe it."

William pursed his lips for a moment. "Ugly thing. A red and green devil, but with a pink ribbon around it. Not the sort of thing we should have at the office," he said distractedly.

Emily swayed. "That's the tattoo I remembered from the night of the accident. Of the man who took Joshua. His name is Frankie."

"Frank Mangino," William said, lips pursed. "I think Eric found out he was stealing from us and threatened to fire him. Frank retaliated by trying to kill all of you and stealing the baby for his sister who couldn't have kids. I didn't know Eric was trying to deal with this alone, Emily," William said earnestly. "I swear I didn't know."

Could that have been why Eric had become so distant?

He'd discovered a man embezzling from the company? She leaned against William as he escorted her to the car. The cold whipped her cheeks. She glanced back to the police station. Was this why Victoria hadn't wanted Emily in the room?

"May I borrow your phone? I need to text Mitch and let him know where I'm going," she said, her voice faint. "He can meet us."

"Sure," William said, his smile eager. "But I've got a ton of passwords. Can't be too careful these days. Give me his number and I'll program it." He opened the door of his BMW for her.

Emily slipped into William's vehicle and waited impatiently as William slid in beside her and set up Mitch's number. Her hands shook as she took the phone and tapped out the message.

She tried to hit Send. A password request popped up. She passed the phone to him, and he gave her a small smile. "Sorry." William typed in a few keys. "Okay, done."

Emily wriggled against the plush leather seats. She couldn't believe it. If what William said was true, she was going to see her son again. William seemed so convinced. She wished Mitch were here, but she couldn't wait to see his face when he saw her with Joshua in her arms. Everything would be okay. "William, thank you for what you've done."

"Father and the adoptive family should be arriving at the Wentworth corporate airport about the time we get there." William smiled gently and patted her hand. "Let's go find Joshua."

MITCH LEANED BACK AGAINST the wall and stared in exasperation at Victoria. "No more games. Who in the family business could authorize that type of money transfer, Mrs. Wentworth? Could you? Your name is listed on a lot of corporate accounts and checks. Why?"

Victoria rubbed her temple. "I received my MBA before I married Thomas. I was the Chief Financial Officer when we first started out." She looked up at Mitch. "When the company went through a rough patch about fifteen years ago, my husband pushed me out of my position, but I'm still a partner."

Mitch picked up the records Victoria had provided and poked at one of the highlighted numbers. "You do realize you've given us enough information to arrest your husband and son." Mitch studied the woman whose elegant persona had started to crumble. Shadows rimmed her eyes. Her makeup looked caked on, not the perfect mask he'd noticed the last time they'd met. "Why are you really here?"

The woman sitting in front of him lifted a devastated gaze. "Eric." She shook her head slowly. "I was certain Emily had killed him. She had the account. I was going to prove it, but I discovered Eric had money stashed away that no one knew about. He opened the account in her name, just before his death. He probably didn't have time to tell anyone before—" She dabbed her eyes. "Then I found the ledgers." She placed her finger next to one of the numbers. "Do you see that mark? That's Eric's mark. He knew about the money transfers."

"So Eric was involved?"

She shook her head vehemently. "My Eric would never do such a thing. But my husband and William, they would do anything to keep the business successful."

Mitch glanced at Tanner, who gave him a slight nod. They were thinking the same thing. Eric Wentworth had known or found out about the money laundering and wanted to stop it. His call to Tanner, as lead detective for white-collar crime, likely had gotten him killed.

What didn't make sense was the connection to Joshua's disappearance.

Mitch leaned forward. "Mrs. Wentworth? Do you know

anyone with a red and green tattoo, perhaps with a pink ribbon? It would stand out."

"Why, yes." Victoria's gaze widened. "The young man who works as my son William's right-hand man has a tattoo on his wrist. William makes him wear long sleeves to cover it, but sometimes it shows."

"What's the assistant's name?" Mitch snapped.

"I've only met him a few times," she said, pausing. "Frank. Frank Mangino."

"Frank," Mitch whispered. "Gotcha."

A knock sounded at the door, and a cop stuck his head in. "Sir," he said to Tanner. "You'll want to hear this."

Mitch and Dane exited the room.

"Two bodies just turned up downtown," the cop said quietly. "One had a wrist tattoo."

"Red and green devil tattoo with a pink ribbon," Mitch said, the frustration churning inside of him. Another lead. Dead.

The uniform nodded. "A gunshot wound in the chest and another through the head. The other body was found nearby. Different caliber."

Tanner turned toward him. "Frank Mangino. Bodies are piling up around here. Someone is not taking any chances of leaving witnesses behind."

Someone who believed he could get away with murder. Mitch slammed into the conference room. "Mrs. Wentworth. Where are your husband and son?"

Victoria started at his intrusion, then straightened her back. "Thomas decided at the last minute to take the plane on business today. I don't know where William is."

"How far would your husband and son go to protect themselves, Mrs. Wentworth?" Mitch asked.

Comprehension dawned on her face. "No, it can't be. They

wouldn't have." She sank back into the chair, stunned, her lip trembling. "Please tell me they didn't kill Eric."

Mitch nabbed his jacket and looked at her. "If they did, they'll pay."

Without pausing, Mitch returned to the bullpen. "I need everything we have on Frank Mangino, and I want any of Thomas or William Wentworth's flight plans for yesterday, today and tomorrow," he barked. "ASAP."

"You sound like a real detective, Mitch," Dane said. "What are you thinking?"

"That Emily will never quit until she finds her son. That makes her dangerous." Mitch had a bad feeling. He tore down the hall to the waiting room. Empty. He checked his phone. No messages. She could be searching the databases. He hurried down the hall and flung open another door. Empty. His gut twisted, and he doubled back to the police station's lobby. "Emily Wentworth? Did you see her?" he demanded of the desk sergeant.

"Sure. She left with some guy maybe ten minutes ago. Fancy suit."

Mitch's heart sank. He'd told her she was safe here. He'd been wrong.

Chapter Fourteen

The Wentworths' large, private hangar loomed tall in the distance. Emily could barely contain her excitement. Her entire body felt supercharged. She grinned at William. "We're almost there. I can't believe it. I'm going to see Joshua. Finally." She squirmed in her seat and leaned forward, staring at the horizon. "You're sure it's him, right, William? I don't know if I can take another disappointment."

"Almost one hundred percent positive," William said. "After a year, he's obviously changed, but this whole nightmare will be over soon."

"Does Joshua's adoptive family know he was stolen?" Emily let out a slow breath. "They'll be devastated." Her heart ached for the horror they'd all gone through because of the man who'd killed Eric and stole her son. The terrible thought hit her. "What if they were in on the kidnapping, William? Maybe we should wait for Mitch and the police."

"Don't worry." William patted her hand. "I've taken care of things."

He turned down a road, and the front of the thousand-square-foot hangar, with its huge sliding door, appeared in the distance. She could just make out the snow gathered around in dirty piles against the metal siding. Areas of black ice slicked the tarmac. William slowed as they made their approach.

Emily squinted. "What's that lying in front of the building?"

The hangar grew closer, and the black blob started to take on the recognizable shape of a man. The gray-haired figure struggled to rise, then waved at them.

Recognition ricocheted through her. Emily gasped. "I think it's your father."

Thomas Wentworth rolled to his side. His chest was bloody.

"William, he's hurt! Hurry!"

Her brother-in-law pressed down on the gas. The car lurched forward.

Emily clenched her fists, and her nails bit into her palms. Who could've hurt Thomas? Had the adoptive family been involved the whole time? Panic clutched her heart. "What about Joshua? Where is he? I don't see anyone else." Frantically, she searched for any other car or movement.

Then she noticed Thomas struggling. He held something in his hand and was pointing it at the speeding car. "Gun!" she yelled.

William wrenched the wheel to the left, just as the front windshield shattered. The car rammed into the side of the hangar and both airbags exploded, turning the world white. Seconds later, everything shuddered to a stop.

Emily shook her head to clear her vision, then released her safety belt and rammed her shoulder against the door until it opened. She had to find cover before Thomas opened fire again. She peeked over the edge of the window. Her father-in-law had fallen back, lying still as death. "He's not moving. Are you all right, William?"

Her brother-in-law groaned and pushed away from the steering wheel and the deflated airbag. His shoulder oozed blood. "No, dammit, I've been shot."

She reached into the car for his phone. "Give me your cell. I'll call for help."

"Leave it alone!" William slammed his fist into Emily's face. Her head snapped back, and her jaw exploded with pain.

"This is all your fault. You ruined everything. You just kept coming and coming, never giving up. You were supposed to be dead. You were all supposed to be dead."

William struggled out of the car, getting caught up in the mangled metal of the hangar door and the BMW. He let out a string of curses as Emily scrambled out the door. Only one place to hide. She bolted for the hangar, hoping there would be a phone inside. Her mind whirled in disbelief. William? She couldn't believe it. Was Joshua even here, or had he lied to get her here and kill her?

"Emily," a weak voice called out from at least ten feet away.

Thomas. She hesitated and crouched beside the car.

"Save Joshua, Emily. He's inside the hangar. Save—"

William stalked over to his father and aimed a Glock at Thomas's head. "Don't die easily, do you?"

"Why did you do this? Your own brother? Your nephew?" Thomas's voice was weak and disbelieving.

"Eric called the cops. Someone had to take the fall, Father. They still do, and it won't be me."

"No!" Emily screamed.

William pulled the trigger.

She scrambled to her feet and raced to the hangar. Was Joshua really in there?

"Don't bother running, Emily," William said. "I have a spot picked out for you. I know exactly where you have to die to make my story stick."

She wouldn't let him win. Not after coming this close. She yanked open the metal access door and fell inside next to the Wentworths' limo. She turned and locked the dead bolt just as William banged against the outside. Curses rained through the metal. Frenetically, she scanned the huge building for Joshua. He had to be here somewhere, but she could only see the plane and the limo and a lot of equipment. Where was her son?

She didn't have much time. She needed help. She needed Mitch. Surely he'd received her text by now.

Unless William had never sent it.

Oh, Lord, of course he hadn't. She had to find a way out, until somehow Mitch figured out what had happened. He wouldn't give up. He'd fight for Joshua. She'd never seen anyone as intuitive and smart as Mitch Bradford. Whatever story William told, Mitch would see through it. He would believe in her. He would uncover the truth.

She just wished she'd told him she loved him. She'd been reluctant and afraid. Now it was too late.

Unless she fought back.

She could do this. Heart pounding, she shoved a heavy metal tool bin against the door and pushed some barrels behind it.

Another shot rang out and pinged near the lock. How long would her barricade keep him out?

A baby howled from inside the limo.

Emily stilled, afraid to move, afraid to breathe. What if…? She raced to the limo, terrified the wonderful, heartbreaking sounds of the baby's cries would vanish like her morning dreams. She threw open the door. The smell of blood and death gagged her. A man and a woman sat motionless in the front seat, eyes sightless. Each had taken a bullet to the head.

Oh, no. Emily's knees quivered.

Another howl wailed.

She could breathe again.

Emily peeked into the back and saw a diaper bag, then a

car seat with an angry little boy in a snowsuit, waving his chubby arms and legs as he furiously tried to escape.

Beneath his stocking hat, he had brown hair. Like Eric's. And the same stubborn chin.

His deep blue eyes. Just like hers.

Her entire body shaking, Emily tugged on the back door. Her hands wouldn't work; her body could barely function. Finally the door opened, and she reached inside. "Joshua?"

The baby stopped crying and stared. Emily's heart paused with uncertainty as his wary gaze transformed into a smile. The dimples were all his own. They always had been.

"It's you." She couldn't stop the tears from rolling down her face.

Another shot rang out, this time at a side door she hadn't blocked.

The baby screamed in fear. "Don't worry, Joshua. Mommy will save you."

Her hands trembling, she shoved aside the heavy diaper bag, then tugged and pressed at the unfamiliar straps and latches of the car seat. "Come on, come on," she said, frantic now. Just one left. Joshua cried even louder. Why hadn't she waited for Mitch? He would've seen through William.

Another gunshot, and a metal crash sounded from directly behind her. She was out of time. The car seat's straps finally gave in under her hand. She grasped Joshua and turned around slowly.

"You're too late, Emily."

William Wentworth, gun and all, had found his way in.

MITCH FLOORED THE TRUCK and barreled toward the Wentworths' hangar. Thank goodness Sierra was a killer hacker. She'd pulled the data from the traffic cams and placed Wentworth's BMW moving toward their private hangar. The flight plans indicated the Wentworths had taken the plane to Okla-

homa and back. Put that together with Frank Mangino's
sister adopting a baby boy a year ago, and everything fit.
Except Emily was still in danger. It didn't take ten minutes
to kill someone; it took seconds. Emily couldn't be dead. He
wouldn't let himself consider the possibility. She was strong;
she was clever. She would stay alive. She'd know he would
come for her. She had to know.

"You there, Dane?" Mitch said into his earpiece, praying
his boss was close behind him.

"Still a few minutes away. SWAT is scrambling."

Mitch skidded to a stop and jumped out of the truck. He
scanned the area, then ran over to what was left of Thomas
Wentworth. "I can't hold off," he said softly. "I've got a BMW
buried into the side of the hangar. Thomas Wentworth is
dead. Shot twice." Mitch ran the twenty-five feet to the edge
of the building. "The side door to the hangar has been shot
open. I'm going in."

"Be smart," Dane said. "Come out alive."

"Get your butt here and make sure she gets out of this.
You worry about Emily, Dane. Promise me. I don't matter,"
Mitch said.

"We're getting you both out," Dane snapped. "I'm almost
there."

Mitch let out a quick breath. *Focus, man. She needs you.
You love her.*

And he hadn't told her. He'd wanted everything perfect.
He'd wanted to be whole. He'd wanted to find her son and
have SWAT back. He should've just said the words. He loved
her more than the job he'd thought he couldn't live without.
If he got another chance—*when* he got a second chance—he
wouldn't wait.

Mitch drew his weapon, eased toward the open hangar
door and peeked in. His blood went cold.

Emily, standing in front of the open limo door, tears running down her face, rocked a screaming baby in her arms.

William, blood dripping down his arm, held a pistol aimed at Joshua's head. "Give me the kid or I'll shoot through him to get to you. You know I'll do it. I'd prefer him alive, Emily, but I can fabricate a reason why he didn't make it. Either way, I win. The choice is yours. Do you want your son to live or die?"

Mitch slipped inside the door and into position behind a metal bin and three huge barrels that blocked William's view. Moving silently, Mitch crouched down and leaned out farther. He focused on Emily, hoping she would glance his way.

As if she could sense him, she turned her head slightly. Their gazes locked, and he recognized the flash of understanding. She shifted her body slightly, drawing William's attention in the opposite direction. Man, he loved an incredibly brave woman.

Mitch's earpiece clicked once, and some of his tension eased. Dane had arrived. Emily hugged the baby tighter. "Why are you doing this, William? I don't understand. You helped me look for Joshua."

"I thought the boy was dead. What harm could it do to pay a washed-up drunk like Perry to search for clues and keep you busy? But the kid was alive, and that idiot Mangino's sister adopted him. Too many loose ends tying back to me."

"And a ton of dead bodies all over your property doesn't lead to you?" Emily asked incredulously.

"After today, I'll help the police wrap the entire case up in a nice bow. According to the paper trail and forensic evidence I planted, my father hired Mangino. He had Eric killed because my brother threatened to expose the company's money laundering. He murdered Joshua's parents because of the connection to Frank. All perfectly true. Except I've got more guts than my father ever did. I did what I had to do."

"You killed your own father," she said, still unable to fathom William's callousness.

"No, Emily. *You* discovered my father planned to kill the baby next, so you had to protect your son. You grabbed a gun and killed my father, but not before he fatally wounded you. And I, the poor grieving son, rescued my nephew. I'll end up on CNN. Business will thrive. And Joshua will save my reputation and follow in the family business."

"You're sick."

William's face went cold. He took a step forward. "And we're done. Goodbye, Emily."

She shoved the baby into the car. A bullet slammed into the metal beside her head. She whirled around to face William and swung the diaper bag at him, connecting with his gun arm. Most of the bag's contents scattered.

"Mitch, save Joshua!" She swung the bag again, aiming for William's head, hoping the heavy box of diaper wipes would stun him or at least slow him down.

William stumbled backward, roared in anger and aimed directly at her. His trigger finger squeezed just as Mitch dove in front of her.

A gun sounded. Another shot rang out from behind William. Emily closed her eyes, expecting to feel pain.

She didn't. The baby's howls mixed with shouts from inside the limo.

"Mitch!" A deep voice yelled.

Emily opened her eyes to the horrific sight of William slumped to the cement, the entire left side of his head gone. She scrambled to her feet, torn between running to the baby or Mitch. Then, as she watched, he stumbled to his knees in front of her, his chest soaked in crimson.

"No!" Emily fell to the ground and pressed her hand against Mitch's wound. Blood flowed through her fingers. "No, Mitch. Don't do this."

"Calm down, Emily," he rasped between clenched teeth, quirking a smile. "It's a flesh wound. No big deal."

"Don't scare me like that, Mitch Bradford," she said. "Ever again."

"I bet you say that to all the guys who stop a speeding bullet for you, you sweet-talker, you."

Footsteps pounded at them. She turned. "Dane, thank goodness. He's been shot."

Mitch's boss ripped off his shirt, revealing a side laced with scars. He knelt next to Mitch and pressed the fabric against the wound. "You're a magnet for trouble, aren't you, Bradford? You're never going to get back to SWAT at this rate."

"Being a detective must be growing on me, Tanner." Mitch coughed, then cursed viciously. He looked at Emily, his smile calm. "Why don't you go check on your son. I'm fine."

"You're sure you're okay?" She bit her lip, staring at the shirt soaked through with blood.

He smiled and nodded even though he was certain he wasn't. Emily didn't need to know that. Not right now. Breathing became more difficult with each passing second, and his leg… Well, Joshua had a better chance of getting up and walking out of here than Mitch did in the near future.

Emily hesitated, then staggered to her feet. Mitch watched, his emotions overflowing as she raced to the car, wiped the blood off her hands and picked up the squalling baby. Her entire body quaking, she carefully lifted her son into her arms, jostling him and squeezing him tight.

The baby looked at her, his expression curious. She smiled and touched the side of his face. Mitch could just catch her emotion-laden words. "Hello, Joshua. I'm your mommy."

She hugged her son close.

Mitch's eyes stung. He'd done it. With his help, Emily had found her son. She was safe. They both were.

An odd pressure bore down on his chest. He gasped for air, trying to fill his lungs. Spots danced in front of his eyes. He wanted to sleep. Needed to rest.

His eyes closed.

"Mitch." Dane pressed harder against the bloody wound at his chest. "Stay with me, man."

He couldn't move, could barely breathe. "Emily's alive. She has her son," Mitch gasped. "I'm fine."

"Liar," Dane whispered. "Luckily, the medevac is almost here."

Mitch barely heard him or the sound of Emily yelling out his name and a baby's cry. The world faded to black.

THE LIGHT HURT HIS EYES. Mitch opened them and stared at a too-familiar white ceiling. He looked down at his chest, at the tubes entering his body, at the wrap around his leg. Definitely not heaven. "I'm in the hospital again, aren't I? I hate this place."

His voice was hoarse; his entire body felt like it'd been run over by a truck. A fuzzy figure standing at the foot of his bed slowly came into focus. Her light brown hair fell in waves around her face, the light surrounding her like a halo. Emily.

But her arms were empty.

He struggled to sit up. "Joshua," he croaked. "Where—?"

"Shh," she said, hurrying around the bedside and pressing him back against the pillows. "He's fine." She poured him a glass of water. Gratefully, he took a sip. "He's cradled in your father's arms, holding a teddy bear." Emily blinked back tears. "Because of you."

Mitch didn't like the thankful tone in her voice. "I did what anyone would have done."

"You have no idea, do you? How good you really are?"

Mitch squirmed as he glanced away from her shining blue

eyes. He shook his head. "I made too many mistakes. I lied too many times."

Emily rose from the bed and walked to the door. She opened it and whispered. A few seconds later, she returned to his bedside, a small boy on her hip, a boy with eyes the color of Emily's.

He swallowed back the emotions that threatened to overwhelm him. This was a picture he'd longed to see for so very long. Emily with her son, at peace, happy. Mitch wanted to take them both into his arms and have them hug him, tight, as if they would never let him go. He wanted to feel her against him. He wanted her son to laugh up at him and smile. "I'm glad for you," Mitch said softly.

"You saved us both," she said. "I have him back because of you. Not because of the cop you are, but because of the man you are. You never gave up. You believed in me when no one else did. You stood by my side. That's more than I could've hoped for."

Mitch sucked in a shuddering breath. He didn't want gratitude. He wanted so much more. But how could he expect her to love him? "Please don't say you're grateful. I couldn't stand that, Emily."

"I'm grateful to Dane for being there for us in the end." Emily sat beside the bed and dangled a small stuffed animal dressed in a policeman's uniform in front of her son. The bear had one blue eye and one brown eye. "I'm grateful to Noah for tossing his money for a rush DNA test to prove to the world that Joshua is my son. I'm even grateful to Victoria for finally admitting the truth to the police and herself. She helped you save my life, and hopefully we can start over. Mostly, I'm grateful to your father for helping us and raising a son like you." She met his gaze. "But I don't feel for them what I feel for you." She cupped his cheek. "I love you, Mitch Bradford."

He closed his eyes, his heart exploding with joy. But at the same time, doubts washed through him. "How?" he muttered. "After everything—"

She pressed her fingers against his lips. "You did what you did to protect me. Just like I'd do anything to protect Joshua. Actions prove much more than words." She hugged her son to her. "Because I love him."

"I don't know if I deserve you, Emily, but I can tell you I won't lie to you again. I won't betray you." As Mitch spoke, Joshua turned to the deep voice. The baby's eyes blinked at Mitch. Joshua grinned, holding his arms out.

"He wants you," Emily said softly. "He trusts you." She bent down and kissed Mitch's lips, gently, sweetly. "Just as I do. I love you, Mitch. For your bravery, your determination, your loyalty. Because even if this had been another Florida—" she kissed her son's head "—I know you'll always be there for me. No matter what."

Mitch held out his hand to her son. Joshua grasped his finger and gave Mitch a toothy grin. His heart melted. "I'm not the man I used to be. I'll never be SWAT again," he warned. "I probably don't have a job after this."

"Do you think your injuries matter to me? Or to Joshua?" She laid her hand on his chest. "I fell in love with the man you are inside. I fell in love with your heart and soul and mind."

The dark cloud encasing Mitch's spirit broke free. He pulled Emily toward him and buried his face in her neck. "I love you," he whispered. "I've loved you forever."

She turned her lips to his, and he kissed her with every promise deep within him. His heart raced as she let out a small groan against him. She pulled away, her eyes sparkling with joy, her breathing fast. "I want you well soon, so you can fulfill the promise of that kiss, Officer Bradford."

A tentative knock sounded at the door.

"Is it safe to come in?" Dane Tanner pushed open the

door. He walked in, leading a parade of Ian, Noah, his other brother, Chase, and his sister, Sierra.

Lastly his father wheeled into the room. "So, Mitchell. You finally got the job done right," his father barked, the intensity belied by the relief in the older man's eyes.

"Hardly," Dane said, stepping forward. "He went against direct orders. More than once."

"He blew up his car," Chase and Ian chimed in together.

Noah crossed his arms and gave Mitch a half-frustrated grin. "He got my SUV shot to pieces."

Sierra ran across the room and kissed her brother on the cheek. "He almost got himself killed more than once." She scowled. "Don't ever do that again, big brother."

"If you'd just waited," Dane said, his expression unsmiling. "I could've made the shot before things got out of hand. Instead, you had to go all hero. Again."

"Are you saying I'm fired?" Mitch asked.

His boss looked him over. "Do I look like a fool? You did a slam-dunk job, Mitch. I don't know anyone else who could've followed those leads. You've got instincts. In fact, I think you're a better detective than you ever were at SWAT entry."

Mitch stared at his boss, stunned, and clutched Emily's hand. "I'm not fired?"

"You may want to quit, but if you want a job on my unit, it's yours for the taking." Dane gave him a small salute. "As long as you work on following procedure a little better in the future."

"That'll be the day," Noah said. "So, little brother? Did you fix things?" He nodded toward Emily.

"Did you grovel?" his father asked with a wink.

Mitch took Emily's hand in his and kissed her palm. "Dad, everyone. Meet Emily and Joshua Wentworth. We're going to be a family."

At the loud shout of approval, Joshua let out a squeal. Noah grabbed his soon-to-be nephew and threw him up in the air, then caught him in his arms. The boy giggled and wrapped his arms around Noah's neck.

Mitch laughed and tugged Emily close. "You'll marry me, right?" he said softly in her ear.

She turned her face, her lips hovering over his. She met his gaze, and Mitch's breath caught at the love in her every feature. She loved him. Truly loved him.

He knew. He believed. He had faith once more.

"I will," she whispered. "Together. Forever."

* * * * *

SUSPENSE

Harlequin®

INTRIGUE®

COMING NEXT MONTH
AVAILABLE APRIL 10, 2012

#1341 SON OF A GUN
Big "D" Dads
Joanna Wayne

#1342 SECRET HIDEOUT
Cooper Security
Paula Graves

#1343 MIDWIFE COVER
Cassie Miles

#1344 BABY BREAKOUT
Outlaws
Lisa Childs

#1345 PUREBRED
The McKenna Legacy
Patricia Rosemoor

#1346 RAVEN'S COVE
Jenna Ryan

REQUEST YOUR FREE BOOKS!
2 FREE NOVELS PLUS 2 FREE GIFTS!

Harlequin®

INTRIGUE®

BREATHTAKING ROMANTIC SUSPENSE

YES! Please send me 2 FREE Harlequin Intrigue® novels and my 2 FREE gifts (gifts are worth about $10). After receiving them, if I don't wish to receive any more books, I can return the shipping statement marked "cancel." If I don't cancel, I will receive 6 brand-new novels every month and be billed just $4.49 per book in the U.S. or $5.24 per book in Canada. That's a saving of at least 14% off the cover price! It's quite a bargain! Shipping and handling is just 50¢ per book in the U.S. and 75¢ per book in Canada.* I understand that accepting the 2 free books and gifts places me under no obligation to buy anything. I can always return a shipment and cancel at any time. Even if I never buy another book, the two free books and gifts are mine to keep forever.

182/382 HDN FEQ2

Name	(PLEASE PRINT)	
Address		Apt. #
City	State/Prov.	Zip/Postal Code

Signature (if under 18, a parent or guardian must sign)

Mail to the Reader Service:
IN U.S.A.: P.O. Box 1867, Buffalo, NY 14240-1867
IN CANADA: P.O. Box 609, Fort Erie, Ontario L2A 5X3

Not valid for current subscribers to Harlequin Intrigue books.

**Are you a subscriber to Harlequin Intrigue books
and want to receive the larger-print edition?
Call 1-800-873-8635 or visit www.ReaderService.com.**

* Terms and prices subject to change without notice. Prices do not include applicable taxes. Sales tax applicable in N.Y. Canadian residents will be charged applicable taxes. Offer not valid in Quebec. This offer is limited to one order per household. All orders subject to credit approval. Credit or debit balances in a customer's account(s) may be offset by any other outstanding balance owed by or to the customer. Please allow 4 to 6 weeks for delivery. Offer available while quantities last.

Your Privacy—The Reader Service is committed to protecting your privacy. Our Privacy Policy is available online at www.ReaderService.com or upon request from the Reader Service.

We make a portion of our mailing list available to reputable third parties that offer products we believe may interest you. If you prefer that we not exchange your name with third parties, or if you wish to clarify or modify your communication preferences, please visit us at www.ReaderService.com/consumerschoice or write to us at Reader Service Preference Service, P.O. Box 9062, Buffalo, NY 14269. Include your complete name and address.

HI11B